SERENDIPITY

Gallipoli: A Love Story

By
G S WILLMOTT

Author's Previous Titles

The Other Side of the Trench – The Spirit of War

Brothers in Arms

Escape – True Accounts of POW Escapes

Red Lights on the Somme

You Forgot the Sauce – An Alzheimer's Journey You Won't Forget

Survival – An Americans Family's Odyssey Through Two World Wars

Boy's Own War – Boy Warriors Fighting Through the Ages

ALL THINGS MUST PASS   3
YOUR COUNTRY NEEDS YOU   11
INTO THE VALLEY OF DEATH   23
PRISONER OF CHUNUK BAIR   31
THE PRODIGAL DIGGER   45
MUSTAFA ATATURK   51
GEOFFREY BECOMES A TURK   51
WAR ENDS   57
GOZDEN IRAK, GONULDEN DE IRAK OLUR.   61
WHERE THERE IS LOVE THERE IS LIFE.   66
FATHER OF MODERN DAY TURKEY   76
THE BUILDING OF AN EMPIRE   82
DIPLOMACY   88
HITLER'S FUN & GAMES   99
PATRIARCH OF THE TURKS   107
HITLER'S MARCH TO WAR   116
I LOVE PARIS   124
EXODUS   129
ROAD TO NOWHERE   135
PLANNING HITLER'S DEMISE   141
I DO LIKE A DAY BESIDE THE SEASIDE   146
TURKEY ENTERS THE WAR   155
I STILL CALL TURKEY HOME   161
WHITE HORSE BLACK DOG   174
CATHARSIS   176
THE BATTLE   183
A HEAVY CROSS TO BEAR   189
GALLIPOLI REVISITED   199
LONELY AND BLUE   205
THE AFTERMATH   207
EPILOGUE   208

All Things Must Pass

Chapter 1

April 25, 1963

ANZAC Day

Franklin Tasmania Australia

The old woman sat in her chair, the only piece of furniture she had in her room; she was reading a telegram she had received from Queen Elizabeth congratulating her on her 100th birthday. She slowly rose out of the chair retrieving a shoebox from her wardrobe; it was in this old cardboard box she kept her most treasured possessions. She folded the telegram placing it in the box to be cherished along with the other cards she'd received since 1918.

One of the nursing home carers knocked on Vera's door; entering, she invited the centenarian to join her friends for morning tea in the dining room.

'Hello Vera, it's time for morning tea darling, come on I'll wheel you down.'

'It better not be a birthday celebration; I've got nothing to celebrate.'

'Don't be like that, you've reached a milestone in your life you should be excited.'

'Excited, why, I'm old, I can't shower myself let alone go to the toilet without somebody there to help me. I'm ready to go up or down, I don't particularly care where.'

'Come on Vera you don't mean that, all your friends are waiting to celebrate your birthday.'

'What friends?'

'Everybody here is your friend.'

'Bullshit.'

'Vera, I've never heard you swear before.'

'Well, you bloody well have now. Don't tell Rabbi Bloomfield.'

'If that's how you feel I'll cancel it.

'Good, now if you don't mind, I'd like to rest.'

The nurse left the grumpy old woman to herself; it wasn't long before Vera buzzed the nurse's station, Julie returned.

'I've changed my mind can you wheel me down?'

'Good, come on let's get you in the wheelchair. I didn't cancel your birthday cake.'

Julie wheeled the birthday girl down to the dining room where the twenty other residents were waiting, not necessarily to sing the birthday song but to receive a piece of birthday cake.

Nevertheless, when Vera made her grand entrance they all burst into song; Happy Birthday to you.

Vera nodded and asked for a piece of cake, once she devoured her second piece she asked Julie to return her back to her room.

'OK Vera let's go, did you enjoy your birthday party?'

'The cake was a bit dry for my liking.'

'Oh, I'm sorry to hear that.'

The nurse sighed to herself, nothing would make this one happy.

A nurse appeared out of another resident's room.

'Julie I need your help, Mr Osborne has fallen heavily, I can't get him onto the bed alone.'

'Ok, Vera I'm going to leave you here for a little while. I need to help nurse Hall, is that all right?'

'I suppose so but don't take too long, I need to go to the toilet.'

Julie followed her colleague into Mr Osborne's room; he was on the floor next to his bed. He was a big man, it certainly required two people to lift him up back onto the bed. Once they accomplished their task Julie returned to where she had left Vera.

'Right darling, let's get you back to your room, are you all right?'

Vera didn't answer.

'Vera is everything ok?'

Still no answer. Julie walked around to the front of the wheelchair. Vera's head had slumped forward, she checked for a pulse, there was none. Once Vera had celebrated her 100th, she decided that was enough time on this earth, time to go.

The nursing home staff made arrangements for the funeral home to collect Vera to prepare her for burial.

Mrs Anderson the General Manager of Elder Care checked Vera's personal file to determine who was her next of kin.

She discovered Vera's great-nephew Paul Jacobson was nominated. Paul lived in Brighton Melbourne with his wife Cheryl and two sons Ian and Craig. Mrs Anderson rang the telephone number listed in Vera's file.

'Hello, Jacobson Transport, can I help you?'

'Hello, I'd like to speak to Paul Jacobson please.'

'Can I ask what it is regarding?'

'Yes, this is Margaret Anderson General Manager of Elder Care in Franklin Tasmania. It's a personal matter.'

'I'll put you through; please hold.'

'This is Paul.'

'Hello Paul this is Margaret Anderson from Elder Care in Franklin Tasmania.'

'Hello Margaret, is Aunty Vera OK?'

'I'm afraid I have some sad news, Paul; your Aunt passed away today.'

'Oh, that is sad, it was her 100th birthday today. I was going to call her.'

'Would it be possible to travel down here to sort through her personal items?'

'Yes of course. I'm the executor of her will, there will be a few things I will need to sort out. I was Aunty Vera's only living relative so I would imagine her funeral will be a small affair.'

'Yes, her few friends at the home would be the only ones to attend. We have a chapel here if you would like to use it.'

'Yes, that would be convenient, thank you, Margaret.'

'Paul, please let me know your plans so I can make sure I'm available when you arrive down here.'

'I will as soon as I've booked my flights.'

Paul drove home at 4 pm, very early by his standards; his wife was surprised to see his Mercedes enter the garage.

He opened the back door greeting his wife with a kiss.

'What are you doing home so early did you lose your job?'

'Hardly, I own the company, remember?'

'A figure of speech darling.'

'Aunty Vera died today; it was her 100th birthday.'

'Oh, I'm sorry to hear that Paul.'

'Yeah, but what a life, I don't think I'll make it to 100.'

'You never know. When's the funeral?'

'I don't know yet, but I'll fly down for it, I need to sort out her personal things.'

'Do you want me to come?'

'No darling, I'll just fly down and back in a day.'

Elder Care notified Paul that Vera's funeral would be held on the Monday of the following week in the nursing home's chapel. Rabbi Bloomfield from the Hobart Synagogue would be conducting the service. He made the appropriate arrangements to fly to Hobart where he hired a car to drive the forty-five minutes to Franklin in the Huon Valley.

The funeral was at 2 pm. He arrived at midday and made his way to the general office where he met Margaret Anderson.

'Hello, Paul I'm glad you could make it, Vera would have been pleased.'

'It's the least I could do Margaret, I regret not visiting her more when she was alive.'

'Don't feel bad Paul, she thought the world of you.'

'Would it be possible to visit her room? I'd like to collect her things please.'

'Yes, of course, although she didn't have many possessions, her most cherished item was an old shoe box full of greeting cards.'

They both headed to Vera's room at the end of the corridor. Upon entering Paul was taken aback with the beautiful view of the Huon River and the mountains beyond.

'I'll leave you here to sort through her things. The service begins at 2 pm.'

He looked in his grand auntie's wardrobe: a few dresses, and a dressing gown was hanging up; shoes, three pairs, neatly placed on the floor. On the top shelf was an old shoebox.

'So this must be her treasure,' thought Paul.

He reached up and grabbed it; he sat down in the wingback chair. Inside the box were cards and a telegram from the Queen. Paul opened a birthday card.

25th April 1920.

Happy Birthday Mother
Thinking of you
Your Loving Son
xoxo

He opened another, this time a Christmas card.

25 December 1922

Merry Christmas Mother and Father
Thinking of you both
Your Loving Son

Paul read another thirty cards, all were short and sweet, all signed by "Your Loving Son."

What son? George, Paul's father, was Vera's only other son, he died when Paul was five years old. Geoffrey was "Missing in Action" at Gallipoli, he was Aunty Vera's eldest son. The likelihood of Geoffrey still being alive would have to be remote but who's been sending cards to Vera all these years?

Paul was determined to find out; whoever sent Vera these cards was obviously very close to his aunt.

He took the box with him, the remainder of her possessions he asked to be donated to Vincent de Paul.

Paul entered the chapel at 1.55 pm. There were a few elderly people seated, one man who looked to be in his sixties and dressed immaculately was on his own. He had olive skin with silver hair and piercing dark brown eyes.

'Who could he be?' thought Paul.

The Rabbi began the service.

At the end of the service, Paul approached the man hoping to discover his connection to Vera.

'Hello, my name is Paul, Vera was my Great Aunt.'

'Hello, my name is Emir.'

'That's unusual name, where are you from Emir?'

'Turkey.'

'May I be so bold as to ask you how you knew my aunt?'

'It's a very long story if you have the time to listen.'

'I'll make the time, why don't we have dinner together? I believe the pub has an excellent restaurant, we can talk there.'

'If you wish, I have some business to take care of first, I suggest 7 pm?'

'Yes, that suits me.'

Paul asked Margaret if he could use the telephone, he needed to call the airline and his wife to let her know he would be staying overnight. He drove to the Lady Franklin Hotel and booked a room for the night. Paul decided he needed a scotch before dinner so the salon bar was his next destination. After two whiskies Paul decided to go up to his room and look through the cards in the box again.

He emptied the box creating two piles; one for Christmas cards the other for birthday cards. Arranging the cards in chronological order he discovered that a card had been sent every year from 1918 right up until her 100th.

Paul entered the hotel dining room. He could see Emir sitting at a table for two next to the open fire.

'Good evening Emir.'

'Good evening Paul, please sit down. I have just ordered a beer, would you like to join me?'

'Yes, why not. Thank you.'

The waitress brought them their drinks.

'So Emir, do you live in Australia now?'

'No, I'm just visiting. I flew over last week to visit Vera on her 100th birthday, it was just serendipitous that I was here when she passed away.'

'So you must have been very close to my Great Aunt, it's a very long was from Turkey.'

'Vera was my mother.'

Paul's jaw dropped. He couldn't believe what he had just heard. 'She was your mother? How could that be? She had two sons, Geoffrey who was killed in Turkey... Oh my God you're Geoffrey aren't you?'

'I have to admit I am.'

'But why didn't you come home after the war?'

'I did in 1956, I wanted to see my mother before she died. My wife and I travelled to Tasmania for that express purpose. However, we didn't get to see her.'

'Why not?'

'She had come down with the flu as had most of the residents. My mother was taken to the hospital in Hobart. The doctors refused us permission to see her for fear of infection. Apparently, it was a very dangerous and infectious strain.'

'You must have been disappointed, it was a long way to come without seeing her.'

'Yes, it was very disappointing. The only positive thing about the trip was I got to show Zehra Tasmania as well as attend the Olympics in Melbourne. We also stayed in Sydney for a few days.'

'I take it Zehra is your wife.'

'That's right, we were married for nearly 40 years.'

'That's a long time, you say "were"?'

'Yes, Zehra died two years ago.'

'I'm sorry to hear that.'

'I miss her terribly.'

'I can only imagine. Do you have children?'

'We had a son, sadly he died young.'

'So, you only had your mother. How have you been able to keep aware of her health from Turkey?'

'I have someone here who keeps me informed.'

'At Elder Care?'

'Yes.'

'So, I'm keen to hear your story.'

'As I said to you earlier, it's a very long story, but if you are willing to listen, I'll tell you.'

'I assure you, you have my full attention.'

Your Country Needs You

Chapter 2

October 1914

The day was hot, 100 degrees Fahrenheit; the Huon Valley in Tasmania didn't usually reach such temperatures even in summer. Geoffrey had travelled into Huonville to purchase some fencing supplies to increase the number of paddocks available for his family's dairy herd. The family's landholding in Crabtree was mostly dedicated to apple orchards however his father had decided to supplement their earnings with dairy cows.

Having purchased the wire and fence posts he decided to partake in a couple of cold ales at the pub he entered the public bar, there were a few stools left he sat down next to his good mate Frank Miller.

'G'day Frank, is it hot enough for you mate?'

'Fucking oath mate, I reckon you could fry an egg on the footpath outside.'

'Yeah, she's hot all right.'

'Still, I better get used to it.'

'What do you mean mate?'

'I'm heading off to Egypt soon.'

'Did you sign up?'

'Yeah, I thought I'd better do my duty for King and country, besides I wouldn't mind seeing a bit of the world. It'll probably be the only chance I'll get.'

'Geez mate you're making me feel a bit bad.'

'Well, why don't you come with me? All you've got to do is walk down to the enlistment centre and sign up.'

'I might just think about it.'

'Don't take too long, I'm heading off to training camp in a few weeks.'

'Where about?'

'They're shipping us across to Melbourne, some place called Broadmeadows.'

'I'll think about it. See you later, I better get this fencing gear home before dark.'

'See you mate. I hope you decide to enlist, we'd have a great old time together.'

'I said I'd think about it.'

Geoff left the pub, checked the ropes holding his load and commenced the half hour drive home along the Huon Road to Crabtree.

That night at dinner he didn't speak much, he was reflecting on the decision he had to make. He washed the dishes, his younger brother George dried, normally there was a lot of chatter between the two of them but Geoff wasn't in the mood. Geoff excused himself and went to his room which he shared with his brother, he laid on his bed and tried to way up the pros and cons. The pro was fighting for his country as well as seeing the world and having a great adventure. The con was leaving his parents to run the property although George was more than capable to help out.

He decided to sleep on it, not that he managed to sleep much at all; he rose at 5 am to milk the cows. He knew at that time what he intended to do. Geoff made the excuse to his father that the hardware co-op had short-changed them for one roll of barbed wire. Therefore, he needed to take the truck back into town that afternoon. He parked the vehicle close to the enrolment office took a deep breath and entered the building. Inside was two desks with an Australian flag hanging on the wall, there was also various recruitment posters scattered around the office. Geoff approached one of the army officers requesting information on how to enlist.

'Take a seat young man and we'll get you sorted. What's your full name?'

'Geoffrey Samuel Jacobson.'

'What's your age?'

'20.'

'What's our occupation?'

'Farm Labourer'.

'What are your parent's names?'

'George and Vera Jacobson.'

'Right, check the details are correct and sign on the bottom of the form.'

'So that's it?'

'Just one more thing, we need to give you a quick medical check up but by the looks of you there shouldn't be a problem.'

Geoffrey was required to strip down to his underwear and undergo a medical examination by the army medic.

'So you measure up all right; I just need to note you have a tattoo on the left side of your neck.'

'It's not a tattoo sir, it's a birthmark.'

'Bloody hell I would have sworn it was a tattoo of a cross. I thought you must have been extremely religious.'

'That's what everybody thinks, they used to call me Jesus at school.'

'Well, I need to note you have a birthmark in the shape of a cross for identification purposes.'

'I hope I don't need to be identified by my birthmark.'

'You'll be OK son.'

Geoff passed the medical with flying colours, he was assigned to the 15th Battalion and ordered to report for basic training in Hobart in fourteen days. He would then sail to Melbourne and onto Broadmeadows army camp for six weeks basic training.

He drove home rehearsing in his mind how he would break the news to his mother and father. He parked the truck in the machinery shed; George was stacking firewood. Geoff approached him and divulged his news.

'You didn't you bastard. It's not fair, I'm too young to join up. You're going off on adventure of a lifetime leaving me to carry the can.'

'Don't worry George, they reckon the war will be over by Christmas. I may not even get to go overseas let alone fight the bloody Germans or Turks or whoever else they throw at us.'

'When are you going to tell Mum and Dad?'

'I suppose tonight at dinner, if I don't you'll probably blurt it out.'

'No, I won't.'

Dinner was always at 6 pm come rain or shine; Vera had baked a roast, the men's favourite meal.

Vera served dinner out to her family. After the meal and tea had been poured Geoffrey announced his news.

'I have something to tell you both.'

'What is it son?'

'I enlisted today.'

'You didn't, why?' asked Vera.

'I felt it was my duty.'

'Your duty is here in the orchard, how do you expect us to cope while you are away playing soldiers?' said Vera.

'I'll hardly be playing, Mother.'

Vera left the room heading for her bedroom where she could cry in private; it wasn't the fact that Geoffrey was leaving the orchard so much she was worried about her eldest son going to war.

Harry, Geoffrey's father, suggested they go outside to the veranda for a cigarette; George remained inside washing and drying the dishes.

'You haven't said anything, Dad, what are your thoughts?'

'If I was your age son I'd be doing the same thing. Just make sure you learn how to shoot straight and keep your bloody head down, your mother and I want you back home in one piece.'

'Thanks, Dad I appreciate your support.'

The day arrived when Geoffrey, Frank and twenty other fine young men from the Huon Valley were loaded onto a bus and transported to Constitution Dock. Waiting for them was the HMAS Melbourne. The Bass Strait crossing was very rough, many of the recruits suffered from sea sickness. On arrival at Victoria Dock, they boarded a train to Broadmeadows.

Broadmeadows was horrible, a wet, muddy quagmire with disease rampant and morale low. What these new recruits didn't know was these conditions put them in good stead for what they were about to face.

After basic training the new soldiers were ready to go to war – well that was the plan.

Geoff, Frank and the remainder of the 15th Battalion were taken by train to Albany Western Australia where they boarded the HMAT Ceramic.

HMAT Ceramic

The voyage was no different from any of the other troop voyages to Egypt. The soldiers endured rough seas, seasickness and boredom, the only relief was playing two up, a gambling game played with two pennies.

The 15th Battalion arrived in Alexandria and then moved to Mena camp where they camped for six weeks. Apart from the usual marching in exhausting heat and rifle practice, the boys partook in some tourist activities such as climbing the great pyramid and taking camel rides. In the evenings many took advantage of Cairo at night; some paid the price for their lustful adventures.

9th April 1915 Egypt

Frank walked into Geoff and John's tent. John was the third soldier to occupy their salubrious accommodation. They were both lying down on their stretchers resting after another day of marching in the Egyptian heat.

'Hey, have you heard the news? We're being shipped out tomorrow. Finally, we're going to see some action.'

'Great, it's about fucking time, I'm sick of this bloody sand and heat,' said Geoff.

'Do you know where they're sending us to mate? I suppose it'll be France,' said John.

'The rumour is it won't be France, more likely Turkey.'

'Oh shit, I heard the Turks put up a bloody good fight at the Suez, those bastards know how to fight.'

'Don't worry Johnno, we're up for it, Turks scream just as loud as Germans when they get stuck by a bayonet.' Geoff said.

'Yeah, I suppose you're right beside it can't be any worse than being stuck here.'

The men were ordered to clean their rifles and bayonets in preparation for the action ahead. Most didn't sleep well, they used the time to write letters and postcards back to their families and loved ones back home.

Reveille was at 5 am; they ate breakfast; same old, and then marched to the train station where they boarded a train bound for Alexandria. The four-hour trip was hot and cramped, the Diggers were pleased to get off the bloody thing.

Two troop ships were waiting at the dock; the HMAT Seeang Bee and the Australind. The gang of three boarded the Australind. It was dusk when they finally set sail heading for Moudros on the island of Lemnos; this would be their staging point before landing at Gallipoli.

Moudros was only fifty miles from the Dardanelles where the Anzacs, British, French and Indian troops would launch their attack on the Ottoman Empire. The base was also a major hospital facility where light cases were treated initially. That status would change as the casualties from Gallipoli mounted.

Moudros Harbour 1915

Moudros Camp

The boys were allotted their tents, and the waiting game commenced, each day passed slowly with still no word about when they would finally experience some action. Geoff and his two mates hoped they would be fighting the Turks very soon. Each day the diggers were required to exercise and partake in rifle and bayonet practice as well as marching, fucking marching.

Two weeks passed then, just when they thought they would never get off the island, they received orders to assemble at dockside.

The three diggers marched down to the wharf and embarked onto the Australind where they were packed in like sardines. Although it wasn't summer quite yet it was still bloody hot; 90 degrees.

They set sail for Anzac Cove, and an adventure none would forget.

The 15th Battalion was assigned the role of follow-up; they wouldn't be joining their Anzac comrades from the 9th, 10th or 11th Brigades in the initial morning invasion. They would wait on the troop ship Australind and await the order to land at Anzac Cove.

The three Australian mates watched from the Australind as the boats, full to the gunnels with Anzacs were towed towards the shore carrying the 9th 10th and 11th Battalions to an uncertain welcome. High Command was unsure the level of defence the Turks would mount against the invasion; they'd soon find out.

Anzacs being towed to shore

It wasn't long before the Turks started to shell the Anzac Cove, shrapnel ripped into Anzac flesh and bullets were also doing their fair share of damage. The retaliatory shelling from the Allied armada made for a horrifying light show. Men were dying before they hit the sand, some drowning under the weight of their heavy packs, others were being ripped apart. Anzac Cove began to turn red.

Turks Defending Gallipoli

'Fucking hell, those poor bastards don't have a chance,' said Geoff.

'Don't worry Geoff, they're Anzacs. We'll lose far too many that's for sure, but I bet we'll win the day,' Frank reassured.

'I don't know about you blokes, but I count myself lucky we weren't in the first group,' said John.

'Do you reckon we'll be OK? I mean those poor bastards have taken the worst of it. By the time we get ashore things may have calmed down,' said Geoff.

'I wouldn't bet on it Geoff, I think we'll get a similar welcome,' said Frank.

'Do you blokes ever regret signing up?' asked Geoff.

'Geez we're just about to fight for the first fucking time and you ask that stupid question,' said Frank.

'No, don't get me wrong Frank, I want to be here. Sort of.'

'I know you do mate. Things seem to be getting worse on the beach, the Turks certainly are not letting up,' said Frank.

Three thirty came around, and the officers on board informed the nervous soldiers that they would be boarded onto the landing craft at 4 pm.

'Back home we used to have afternoon tea at four; I used to look forward to a nice cup of tea and one of Mum's homemade scones,' said John.

'Well, you won't be getting tea and scones today mate, you'll be lucky to be eating beef jerky on the beach tonight,' said Frank.

The time came when they were ordered to assemble at the side of the ship where they would be required to climb down rope ladders and into the landing boats.

Anzac Troops preparing to board

Climbing down to the landing craft

The officer in charge of the boarding operation was Captain Humphries, a senior officer who had fought in the Second Boer War. He had a pretty good idea what these young men would face and couldn't help but wonder how many would survive the landing.

It was time for Geoff and his mates to climb the ladder down to the waiting landing boat.

'All right men, down you go. Keep your heads down, I'll see you on the beach,' Captain Humphries reassured.

One by one the soldiers climbed down into the small craft and took their seats. Geoff was assigned an oar while the other two sat in the middle hoping they were in a safe position protected from bullet and shrapnel.

The steamboats towing them took off towards what would become known as Anzac Cove; the noise from the battlefield was deafening.

'Bloody hell John, this is all a bit scary. I hope we get to the beach alive,' said Geoff.

'We'll be right mate, just keep your head low and listen out for bullets coming your way.'

'How the fuck will I know bullets are coming my way?'

'Don't worry son, you'll know.'

About four hundred metres from the beach the steamers cut the row boats loose, Geoff and the other oarsman began to row; they were now close enough for the Turkish machine gun bullets to hit their targets.

Frank hadn't said anything since entering the boat, that was unusual for him.

'Hey Frank, are you all right mate?' asked Geoff.

'Yeah, I'm OK, just a little scared.'

'We all are mate, don't worry about that; fucking hell how could we not be.'

The boat neared the shore, Geoff looked around at the rest of the Diggers in the craft and couldn't believe it, at least ten of the forty who started out on the short journey had been killed, and at least another five or six had severe wounds. He was so intent on his own safety he wasn't aware others had been hit. He was relieved that his two mates hadn't bought a bullet.

Captain Jones gave the order to disembark and run for the bottom of the cliffs where the first wave had established some sort of a beachhead.

Geoff was the first to jump out; he disappeared under the water, which was about five feet deep. The weight of his pack made it very difficult for him to make his way. He finally found a footing and waded towards the stony beach. Once on dry ground he ran as best he could with a wet uniform and a pack that weighed over forty pounds dry; God knows how heavy it was wet. He made it to the cliff without being shot. John and Frank also made it safely. The same could not be said for the rest of the Battalion, over one hundred men either died in the boats or on the beach cut down by a ferocious Turkish defence.

The 15th were instructed to move to the left flank of the beachhead and then to move inland to support their comrades who had landed in the early morning. By the time they began to climb, darkness had descended over the beach bringing a dark curtain over the dead and wounded.

Captain Humphries led his troops up the steep cliff face, the crumbling rock made it difficult to climb. The constant shellfire also contributed to the difficulty of the task.

'For fucks sake Frank, this is getting a little ridiculous, every time I take one step up I fucking slip back two. How in the hell are we going to make it to where ever the fuck we're supposed to be going?' complained Geoff.

'Mate we're all in the same fucking boat, just keep going. There's no going back now.'

Finally, the platoon made it to a valley, which would be later named "Shrapnel Gully" and for good reason.

Into the Valley of Death

Chapter 3

The gully, leading into Monash Valley, became the main supply route of the Anzacs. The troops made their way through the valley and climbed up the steep slopes to man the trench line along the second ridge at positions such as Quinn's Post and Pope's Hill. Transported up the gully went all the supplies essential to holding the line – food, water, engineering supplies and ammunition –while Turkish shrapnel shells exploded overhead.

Supplies Being Moved in Shrapnel Gulley

The men had no time to rest in the gulley, their objective for the night was to reinforce the 10th and 11th in Monash Valley. The Turks had already discovered the Anzac trail and had established several sniper sites. They were camouflaged and lethal, manned by their best sharp shooters.

'Right men, we need to keep going, keep your eyes and ears open there may be snipers above us,' said Captain Humphries.

The Captain had hardly finished his words when a sniper's bullet struck him in the head. He collapsed onto the sandy soil blood gushing from the wound. He was dead by the time he hit the ground.

'Fucking hell, quick dive for cover everyone, there's bound to be more than one of the bastards,' yelled Lieutenant Daley who was now commanding officer.'

As the diggers lay prostrate on the harsh ground hoping a sniper's bullet wouldn't find them next, Geoff turned to his good mate and said.

'Dangerous place mate.'

'Fucking oath it is,' answered Frank.

Lieutenant Daley gave the signal to move on, the Anzacs crept down the valley ever vigilant ever watchful. Although snipers kept up their deadly attack, only one more Digger got hit.

During the next few weeks, the 15th fought the Turks while at the same time they dug a deep communication trench along Monash Valley. Sandbag walls were also constructed to give the men some protection from the Turkish snipers.

Geoff had been identified by Lieutenant Daley to be an excellent marksman. He was chosen to take on a counter sniper's role along with John to act as his spotter using a telescope. The two soldiers would lie out all day observing Turkish sniper positions and firing on them when the least amount of movement was observed. They became known as the best sniper team in the Battalion and were respected by all the men including their commanding officer.

Despite all the precautions that were taken, there were many casualties in Monash Valley.

One of the regular occurrences each day was a private with a donkey ferrying wounded soldiers from the battles in the hills through Monash and Shrapnel Gully down to the medical clearing stations on the beach. He was a very friendly and jovial soul who seemed oblivious to the danger surrounding him. From April 25th until May 19th he saved over three hundred wounded Anzacs.

It was on May 19th that Simpson was shot in the back by a Turkish machine gunner, he died instantly.

Simpson and His Donkey

Anzac Cove Clearing Station 02/05/1915

Geoff immediately responded taking out the machine gun nest.

Private John Simpson Kirkpatrick was born in England in 1892 and was buried in Beach Cemetery Gallipoli.

He was recommended to receive the Victoria Cross posthumously but the British Government denied this Australian request.

Beach Cemetery 1915

The 15th were charged with securing Pope's Hill and Quinn's Post.

Quinn's Post, named after Major Hugh Quinn, 15th Battalion (Queensland) AIF, was one of the most dangerous places on the Gallipoli peninsular. *'Men passing*

the fork in Monash Valley', wrote Charles Bean, *'used to glance at the place as a man looks at a haunted house'.*

Quinn's was positioned on the northern edge of the front line along Second Ridge, just beyond was located Dead Man's Ridge, where Turkish snipers lurked killing many Anzacs. Other Turkish trenches lay opposite; if the Turks could have advanced just a few metres Quinn's, would have been captured and the Anzacs annihilated.

Quinn's Post

Until the end of June 1915, the fighting at Quinn's between Turk and Anzac were ferocious and unrelenting.

Geoff and John took unprecedented risks every day finding the right position to take out the Turkish snipers. The count at the end of May was fifteen snipers although the toll the Turks had amassed was closer to one hundred Anzacs.

The other great threat to life and limb for both sides was hand grenades or bombs as they were called. There was a constant barrage of bombs thrown from either trench causing death and destruction to the belligerents.

'Hey John we seem to be a bit low on bombs mate can you move down and ask munitions for some more?' asked Geoff.

'Right-oh mate, I'll see what I can muster up.'

'Keep your fucking head down cobber or you won't make it ten feet, the bastards are bad today'

'Don't worry about me mate I'll be back with the bombs before you know it.'

The bombs they both referred to were homemade explosives called jam tin bombs. The British had underestimated how many mills bombs would be required so the Anzacs reverted to making their own. The jam tins were filled with gunpowder plus Turkish shrapnel and barbed wire. They were very rudimentary but effective.

The bomb factory was located on ANZAC Cove beach.

AUSTRALIAN WAR MEMORIAL   H10291

ANZAC Bomb Factory

Jam Tin Bombs

John arranged for two hundred bombs and three donkeys plus a private from 16th Battalion to escort him back.

The two soldiers were making their way through Shrapnel Gully when a shot rang out, John dropped to the stony ground blood pouring from his left eye. A sniper had shot him with uncanny precision. Now there were two.

John's parents would receive the infamous telegram four weeks later delivered to the family home in Ballarat, Victoria.

The soldier who had accompanied John, George Russell, continued the dangerous journey without mishap he arrived at Quinn's with his lethal cargo.

'Are you Geoff?' asked George.

'Yeah that's me what can I do for you?'

'I've got two hundred jam tins for you mate.'

'Oh good, we can certainly do with them it's been a bit of a one-way battle going on today. Where's John?'

'He copped one going through Shrapnel Gulley. I'm afraid his dead mate, sorry.'

'Fucking hell, not me good mate John, that stinks.'

'Yeah I didn't know him but he seemed like a good bloke.'

'He was, a bloody good bloke. Did they take him away for burial?'

'I don't know I had to leave him where he fell.'

Prisoner of Chunuk Bair

Chapter 4

6 August 1915

Orders came down from HQ to dispatch a reconnaissance group to try to determine the Turkish strength at the Nek prior to the attack. Geoff was chosen to be one of the four diggers assigned because of his skill as a sharpshooter. The other three were Harry Davis, Jim Bowes, and Anthony Cook. Jim was a corporal and therefore led the band of brothers out into the rough treacherous terrain.

They tried to keep down as much as possible but that wasn't always achievable due to the rough ground.

'OK fellas we've got to be getting close to Abdul's trench line keep your eyes, and ears open.'

They slid on their bellies up a slight ridge they could see the Turks in the trenches and moving around behind their defensive line. They were talking and laughing not what they expected to see. Jim estimated hundreds if not thousands of enemy soldiers just waiting to greet the Aussie diggers.

'There's no way we can take these bastards on we need to get back and tell the lieutenant he needs to let General Hughes know they have to call the assault off.'

'I agree,' said Geoff.

As each soldier turned to retreat they were confronted with a dozen Turkish soldiers each with a rifle pointed directly at them. Their leader, obviously an officer, had a handgun.

Although none of the four understood Turkish, they all had a pretty good idea what was being yelled at them. The Australians lay their weapons down and raised their hands in the air.

'I hope to God they don't shoot us here and now,' thought Geoff.

The diggers were ordered to march to the Turkish line, once reached they were instructed to sit in a circle. The officer indicated that if they spoke they would be shot. After about eight hours the hungry diggers were fed some flat bread and a bean dish, which tasted better than the bully beef they had endured since landing at Gallipoli.

The POWs slept on the ground without blankets none of them slept well. In the morning, they were ordered to join ten other prisoners and march in pairs guarded by four Turkish guards. At 9 am they heard a barrage, it wasn't the Turk's artillery it was the allied warships anchored in the cove. The prelude to the Battle of the Nek had begun without the strength of the enemy's defences known.

The Nek is remembered for the futile tragedy it was, the charge of the Australian Light Horse Brigade and the irresponsible so-called leadership, which was responsible for so many young men's lives.

The original plan had envisaged the New Zealanders attaining Chunuk Bair and then coming down the range behind the Turkish positions towards the Nek. However, this did not happen. Just before dawn the lead New Zealand battalion–the Otagos–were still short of Chunuk Bair. General Birdwood, the commanding officer of the Anzac forces, allowed the light horsemen to give all possible support to the Chunuk Bair assault. If Turkish reinforcements could be held from that vital height for even an extra half hour then its capture, the main purpose of the August offensive, may well be achieved. However, Birdwood had written earlier of the Turkish positions at the Nek and up the slopes of Baby 700:

> 'These trenches and convergences of communication trenches … require considerable strength to force. The narrow Nek to be crossed … makes an unaided attack in that direction almost hopeless.'

At 4.30 am the first wave of the 8th Light Horse Regiment–men from western Victoria–rose from their trenches and dashed for the Turkish line at the Nek. Minutes later a second wave went over. Lieutenant William Cameron, 9th Light Horse, was watching the charge:

> We saw them climb out and move forward about ten yards and lie flat. The second line did likewise … As they rose to charge, the Turkish Machine Guns just poured out lead and our fellows went down like corn

before a scythe. The distance to the enemy trench was less than 50 yards,
yet not one of those two lines got anywhere near it'.

Within half, an hour two further waves–men of the 10th Light Horse from Western Australia–met a fate similar to the Victorians. From his vantage point on the approaches to Chunuk Bair to the north, Sergeant John Wilder of the Wellington Mounted Rifles saw the destruction of the 8th and 10th Light Horse:

'I saw the whole thing … and don't want to see another sight like it.
They were fairly mown down by machine guns.'

Probably the attack on the Nek affected its purpose of holding temporarily near Baby 700 at least part of the Turkish reinforcements which were just then streaming northward towards Chunuk Bair.

The charge at The Nek was the most senseless and tragic waste of Australian lives at Gallipoli.

The hundred and forty Australian lives wasted by two incompetent Australian Officers.

Brigadier General Frederick Hughes and Lieutenant Colonel John Antill.

The Aftermath of the Charge at The Nek

The Nek – Many didn't make it out of the Trench

The New Zealand forces at Chunuk Bair also suffered terribly, with casualties of seven hundred and eleven of the seven hundred and sixty men who held the peak for two days before being relieved by two British battalions. The battalions were subsequently evicted by an Ottoman counter-attack led by Mustafa Kemal.

Meanwhile, troops led by John Monash and an Indian brigade became lost on their way to the Hill 971 objective.

Although the beaches were only lightly defended, the Suvla landing echoed the ANZAC landing in its confusion. Little ground was gained in the first two days, despite enormous casualties, and on the morning of 9 August Turkish reinforcements forced back the attack. The fighting continued until a final British offensive on 21 August at Scimitar Hill and Hill 60.

The POW March – The Nek

The Turks hit the ground, the Australians followed suit. An enormous explosion devastated the immediate area. When the dust settled Geoff couldn't open his eyes. He felt around and discovered somebody's hand, he pulled it to try to get a reaction from its owner the hand and half an arm came away. Eventually, the digger gained his site. He tried to decipher the devastation, there were body limbs scattered around the point of impact. Endeavouring to get to his feet he discovered his left leg had received a severe wound. Geoff found one of the Turkish soldier's rifles, a German Mauser; lying beside him he used it as a crutch.

The wounded digger looked for the other Australians, however, all had been killed. He had been fortunate, being the last man in the line he avoided the full impact of the shell.

The only survivor faced a conundrum, if he tried to return to his own line he would have to pass through the Turkish defences; his chances of surviving were minimal. His other choice was to move deeper into Turkish territory in the hope he would find refuge. He chose the latter option.

The first priority was water, as he hobbled over the impact zone searching for undamaged water canteens he found three. The next priority was food rations, he found enough for four days. Finally he scavenged an ammunition belt hoping he wouldn't need to use it.

Geoff looked down at his leg, it was bleeding heavily. He knew if he didn't stem the flow he wouldn't last the night. Using a singlet he removed from one of his dead comrades he created a tourniquet, it seemed to work however he knew if he didn't get medical assistance he would bleed to death.

He decided to try to keep the coastline in site without being conspicuous. His main objective was to avoid Turkish patrols. He knew most of the Turkish army was somewhat occupied by the ANZACs and other allied troops further up the peninsula, the direction he chose was far from the fighting.

The next critical decision was when to travel, day or night. Despite the obvious danger he chose to walk during the day and rest at night. Where he was actually heading and what he would do when he reached there was a total unknown.

The terrain was reasonably flat, predominantly farmland with the occasional ravine, these ravines would not be difficult to traverse normally, however with an injury such as Geoff's they proved to be very difficult. He managed to stay unnoticed during his first day; he bypassed several fishing villages where he observed men unloading their catch of fish and squid.

'If only I could approach them and ask for a fish how good would that be compared to the shit I have to eat,' he thought.

Geoff knew that would be certain recapture and possible death, he tried to put the temptation out of his mind.

The nights were cold, this made it difficult for the digger to sleep, as he had neither blanket nor heavy coat to keep him warm. He had been walking for three days yet had no idea where he was heading, on the fourth day he discovered a large settlement—he would later learn the town was Tekirdag, the largest population centre on that part of the Turkish coast. Geoff knew he had to avoid the centre despite knowing he may be able to obtain food and water. He moved across the hills overlooking Tekirdag, he observed lights in the distance. The exhausted digger decided he would make for the light source hoping it was a farm and not a Turkish garrison. As he neared, he observed a large house with several outbuildings including a large barn. Geoff knew he needed shelter and a warm place to sleep—if he didn't find it the chances of making it through the night was minimal.

He hobbled towards the barn all the while looking around to ensure there weren't any guards. Opening the heavy doors with difficulty he entered the dry warm building. The barn held farm machinery and hay, lots of hay. Creating a bed from the feed, Geoff felt that he was staying in a fine hotel compared to where he had been sleeping for the past few nights. He slept soundly until the morning when he woke to the sensation of cold metal being pushed against the back of his neck. Slowly he opened his eyes expecting to see a Turkish soldier, instead was a beautiful Turkish woman probably in her early-twenties holding a shotgun.

'Who are you?'

Geoff was surprised she spoke English.

'My name is Geoffrey Jacobson.'

'Are you English?'

'No, Australian.'

'Are you a deserter?'

'No, I was taken prisoner; my guards were killed by a shell I was the only survivor.'

'Were you wounded?'

'Yes, I'm afraid so.'

'I'll look at it but first, put these on your wrist.'

The woman handed him a manacle, he slipped it around his wrist and clamped it as instructed. She clamped the other side around a metal pole next to his improvised bed. Once secured, she examined his leg wound.

'You still have shrapnel lodged in the leg, you are fortunate it didn't sever an artery. I'll need to extract it, or you will lose your leg or worse still, die. I'll be back shortly I need to get some things from the house.'

The Turkish woman returned within fifteen minutes with a leather roll and a bottle of saline solution, bandages and a needle, and thread. She opened the roll; Geoff observed medical instruments including a scalpel.

'I have no ether; you need to be brave.'

The woman first cleaned the wound and irrigated it using the saline liquid, she then used the scalpel to scrape away gravel that had entered the wound.

'OK I need to dig out the shrapnel, this is going to hurt you, you mustn't scream.'

She began to cut the flesh deep in Geoffrey's leg, the pain was excruciating. Finally the woman was able to remove the metal with forceps.

'Australia, I need to stitch the wound. I can't do it alone you need to help me.'

'OK, how?'

'I need you to squeeze the wound together so I can stitch it. Can you do that?'

'I suppose I'll have to, are you going to release me from the manacles? I'll need both hands to squeeze the skin together.'

'You must promise me you won't try to escape.'

'I'm pretty sure I won't be able to walk let alone escape lady.'

'My name is Zehra.'

'Sorry, Zehra. My name is Geoffrey.'

'OK, squeeze the skin together.'

Zehra began stitching the wound. By the time she had finished thirty-two stitches held the wound together. She reattached the manacle and left Geoffrey to rest after his ordeal.

She returned to check on Geoffrey a few hours later. He was sleeping comfortably, Zehra decided not to wake the wounded soldier, she would bring him soup and bread later.

'Geoffrey, are you awake? I've brought you some chicken soup and freshly baked bread.'

'Yes, I'm awake, I just had my eyes closed.'

'Can I help you sit up?'

'Thank you, I'm sorry I've forgotten your name.'

'Zehra, now let's get you up so you can eat your dinner.'

'Dinner? Isn't it still morning?'

'No it's 6 pm, you've been sleeping all day. It's little wonder after what you've been through.'

'My God that's amazing.'

Zehra helped the Australian sit up with his back supported by a bale of hay, another bale acted as a table. Geoffrey finished the soup in minutes, it was the best meal he had since Egypt months before.

'That was beautiful soup Zehra.'

'I'm glad you liked it. We call it Sultan's soup.'

The Turkish woman unwrapped the bandage to check if the wound was bleeding, she was satisfied with the way it looked. She changed the bandage and eased the digger back down to his sleeping position.

'Is there anything else you need before I go?'

'May I have some water please?'

'I filled your canteen this morning, it's beside you.'

'Thank you, I really appreciate your help.'

'Don't be too thankful, as soon as your wound heals I will be turning you over to our army.'

'I understand, this is war and I'm the enemy.'

'Yes, you are, goodnight.'

'Good night.'

'Oh one more thing, what if I need to relieve myself?'

'There's a bucket behind you.'

'Thank you.'

Geoffrey remained in the barn for a further two weeks. Zehra would bring him his meals and water three times a day.

Zehra decided after the second week that the young Australian needed a bath badly, he smelt worse than her pigs.

'You need to bathe, I will undo the manacle but you must promise me not to escape.'

'I give you my word.'

'Why would I try to escape, I have nowhere to go and I get three meals a day here,' he thought.

The young woman unlocked the restraint and led him to the large farmhouse. She guided him to a bathroom where a copper bath was waiting.

'I will unlock the manacle from your wrist, the bathroom will be locked from the other side. You have thirty minutes to bathe yourself. I will bring you a change of clothing, they were my husband's. He was a similar size to you so they should fit.'

'What should I do about the bandages Zehra?'

'Remove them, I will change them after you've bathed.'

The Anzac undressed and removed the bandages. He carefully lowered himself into the warm bath, he couldn't believe how good it felt. Geoff luxuriated in the soapy water for twenty-five minutes, the remaining five minutes was used to scrub his weary body clean. A knock on the door brought him back to reality. Zehra entered and left some clean clothes on a chair in the corner. Also left were shaving gear and a hairbrush.

When the Australian digger emerged from the bathroom he looked like a new man, clean clothes, shaven except for a thin moustache, and his hair brushed back. Zehra was taken aback, she didn't realise how handsome her captive was.

'Geoffrey you look wonderful.'

'Thank you I feel wonderful.'

'I still need to bandage your leg, come with me into the kitchen. Right, would you take down your trousers please.'

'Now there's an invitation I could hardly refuse,' he thought.

Zehra proceeded to examine the wound.

'I think its time to remove your stitches.'

'That's excellent, so it looks pretty good?'

'I wouldn't call it pretty, but yes it seems to have welded together well.'

She unpicked the stitches and rubbed saline solution over the wound.

'I think we should leave the bandage off for now and give it time to breathe. You can pull up your trousers now. Would you like a cup of Turkish tea and a Turkish biscuit?'

'Yes, that would be nice thank you.'

Zehra prepared the sweet tea and placed a plate of Sekepure on the kitchen table.

'Don't you want to manacle me to the table leg?'

'I hope that's unnecessary, are you intending to make a run for it?'

'No, I assure you I'm not. May I enquire where you learnt your medical skills?'

'My husband was a doctor I assisted him, I'm a nurse.'

'I take it your husband is no longer alive you always mention him in the past tense.'

'He was a Medic in the army, a captain, he died on the day you invaded our country.'

'Oh, I am sorry Zehra.'

'I miss him very much he was a kind and loving man.'

'What can I say?'

'Nothing Geoffrey, it wasn't your fault. The futility of war.'

'Have you always lived in this part of Turkey?'

'No I was raised in Istanbul I met my husband while on an archaeological dig at the site of Göbeklitepe.

'Excuse my ignorance, what is Göbeklitepe and where is it?'

Göbeklitepe

'It is located northeast of the Sanliurfa in the south, it was a religious centre, dating back approximately 12,000 years. It is composed of approximately 20 round and oval structures, reaching 30 meters in diameter, six of them have been exposed in excavations. My husband and I were students on vacation assisting in the dig.'

'Zehra, do you mind if I ask you your husband's name?'

41

'Serkan Ozan.'

'That's a very distinctive name.'

'He was a very distinctive man from an important family.'

'Well, I suppose I better return to the barn.'

'I've just gone to all that trouble to get you clean, I don't think the barn is suitable.'

'What do you mean?'

'There's a workman's cottage at the back of the house, you can stay in there.'

'Thank you, that sounds better than the barn I must say.'

The young woman guided Geoffrey to the cottage, it had two bedrooms, a kitchen and living room as well as an inside bathroom. The toilet was out the back.

'I'm not going to restrain you, I will rely on your word not to escape. There's nowhere you can go anyway.'

'I can assure you I will behave myself.'

'The only issue will be if we have visitors, I need to explain your presence. You don't speak or understand Turkish; I suggest we say you are a Turk who fought on the peninsula and became a deaf mute during the heat of battle.'

'What an excellent plan Zehra. I grew up on an orchard and dairy farm, I'm sure I can work around the farm and try to earn my keep.'

'That would be excellent, since the war I have had to do everything myself.'

Life for Geoffrey just got better and better. His leg had healed and he enjoyed helping out around the farm pruning the olive trees and tending the vegetable garden. He was also a handyman, which enabled him to repair many things around the farm and inside the house. He cooked for himself except on Sundays when he joined Zehra in the house. Geoffrey enjoyed these meals, it gave him the opportunity to discuss all manner of things with this very intelligent woman.

The Australian digger began to feel guilty, here he was living in comfortable quarters eating fresh meat and produce on a daily basis while his comrades were stuck in muddy cold trenches eating beef jerky and sipping weak tea. More important they were fighting the Turks and dying like flies. As time went on the more racked with guilt, he became.

December 15, 1915

Emir was sitting at the table with Zehra eating rack of lamb, a popular Turkish dish, accompanied by a glass of French Pinot Noir.

'Zehra, I have something important to tell you.'

'Yes?'

'I know I gave you my word I wouldn't escape, but I feel compelled to go back to Gallipoli and join my comrades. It's my duty as a soldier.'

'So now that you are strong and healthy you wish to return to kill my countrymen?'

'I know it sounds terrible, but I feel I have no alternative.'

'What's to stop me alerting the authorities and have you arrested?'

'Nothing.'

'Let me think about it, I'll give you my answer in the morning. Now, I think you should go.'

'Goodnight Zehra.'

She did not reply.

The following morning Zehra approached Geoffrey's cottage. She knocked on the door he opened it immediately.

'May I come in?'

'Of course Zehra please come in.'

'I have decided to help you return to the peninsula, I thought long and hard, after all you are my country's enemy. I tried to determine what my brother would do in the same circumstances and came up with my decision. It is every soldier's duty to return to the fray no matter what his circumstances, my husband and my brother would have done the same.'

'Thank you Zehra, I didn't know you had a brother.'

'He's an officer in the army. Do you know how to sail a yacht?'

'Yes, I sailed small yachts from the time I was a boy.'

'I will get you to Tekirdag where a yacht will be moored at the jetty. It will be provisioned with three days food and water. You simply sail south until you reach Ari Burnu Cove (ANZAC Cove)'

'I don't know how to thank you Zehra.'

'I'll need a couple of days to get it all organised.'

'Thank you again.'

'You can show your appreciation by finishing the jobs you've been working on before you leave.'

'I will, I promise.'

The Prodigal Digger

Chapter 5

December 18, 1915

Zehra had arranged for the yacht to be ready at the Tekirdag jetty to sail with three day's provisions including water, she also washed the Anzac's uniform so he could dress appropriately prior to his landing at Anzac Cove.

'You simply head south hugging the coastline the whole way, in two or three days you'll reach your destination. Be careful when you enter Tekirdag there is a large garrison stationed in the town, wear your sign saying you're a deaf mute and they should leave you alone. Goodbye, Geoffrey, I'm sorry to see you go.'

'Goodbye Zehra, thank you for saving my life and allowing me to stay with you all this time.'

'Don't throw your life away Geoffrey.'

'I won't I'll keep my head down.'

The Australian began his journey back to the front, after one hour's walk he entered the town of Tekirdag. He headed for the waterfront where he discovered the sixteen-foot yacht tied to the jetty. Geoffrey boarded the vessel, untied the rope, and rowed out into the Dardanelles. Once the point was reached where he felt he was no longer in sight of the garrison, the digger raised the mainsail; the yacht caught the wind heading south. A southerly was blowing at 20 knots making the sailing easy.

Geoffrey sailed through the night, the occasional light shining from the mainland kept him navigating in the right direction. He wished he had a compass, but none was provided. About 4 am he felt safe enough to close his eyes, with the tiller secured the Australian soldier slept for a few hours.

When Geoffrey woke he sighted the small town of Gaziko, that meant he was already halfway to Anzac Cove. This fact lifted his spirits, at the rate he was sailing the yacht would make its objective by the end of the day.

The winds remained favourable. At 5 pm the yacht entered Anzac Cove, however there was something wrong, the beach was normally a hive of activity, but now it was totally deserted. He kept the yacht two hundred yards from shore observing the beach from north to south. The only thing on the sand was a few seagulls and what looked like an enormous amount of debris. He decided to row in and land on the beach, maybe the Anzacs had made tremendous inroads in land and had the Turks on the run.

The perplexed Anzac beached the craft securing its anchor on the stony sand; he alighted and began his walk up the beach. He reflected on the first time he had been on this beach, nothing like what he was experiencing now.

There was abandoned equipment littering the cove, he had to navigate between all manner of military equipment.

ANZAC Cove After Reteat

Geoffrey felt lonely, abandoned; it was quite an eerie feeling, the only Anzac left standing. He walked to the southern end of the cove where he knew the Beach Cemetery was located.

Dressed in his uniform he stood in front of the graves marked with their wooden crosses, all hand painted with the victim's name, battalion, and date of death.

He walked between the graves when one particular cross took his attention:

Private Frank Miller

5th Battalion

Died 1st December 1915–Age 20

Geoffrey froze.

'No, not Frank, fucking hell mate, I told you to keep your fucking head down.'

Geoffrey was devastated, his best mate had been killed and for what reason?

The digger walked away from the cemetery, tears flowing freely down his face. He decided to climb up to the Nek and Lone Pine just to satisfy himself that he truly was the only one left on the peninsula.

He began climbing up past the Sphinx reaching Plugges's Plateau and up through Monash Valley reaching Russell's top within the first hour of walking. The last time he took this route it took over a day.

'Funny how easy it is when you don't have the enemy firing at you,' he thought.

He passed countless ammunition boxes and jam tin bombs along the way. The trenches were full of rubbish, particularly bully beef tins. He hoped he would never have to eat that shit again, the Turkish dishes he had been eating over the past few months had spoiled him.

Geoffrey finally reached the Nek close to the spot where he had been captured. He sat on a rock and looked out over the rugged terrain to Suvla Bay.

Geoffrey's View of Suvla Bay

It was obvious the Allies had retreated from the Gallipoli Peninsula, which left him stranded in a country at war with his own. There was only one alternative, sail back to Tekirdag and ask for Zehra to take him back.

The weary sad digger made his way back to the beach where he paid his last respects to his mate Frank. The lone soldier pushed the little yacht out into the cove and began rowing out to the point where he could raise the sails. The return trip would not be as easy, he would be sailing against the wind, which required constant attention to the sails and sailing on a significant angle, not a direct route. The trip took four days; double the time of his initial voyage. Geoffrey tied the boat to the jetty, he had changed back into his civilian clothes and threw his Anzac uniform overboard. Unfortunately, he no longer had his deaf-mute sign, if Turkish soldiers approached him he'd have to play act his way past them.

Geoffrey was able to pass through the seaside town without incident. He stayed off the road when approaching Zehra's farm so as to avoid any Turkish patrols. Finally he could see the farm in the distance, he started to feel excited at the thought of seeing Zehra again. As he approached the farm he could see Turkish soldiers surrounding the farm, a large Mercedes motor vehicle was parked directly outside her front door. It was obviously a high-ranking officer's car.

Geoffrey was fearful that she had been discovered harbouring an enemy soldier, him. The likelihood of her being shot was high but what could he do? He had no weapon and even if he had a rifle he would be no match for a platoon of Turkish soldiers. He decided to lay low and wait, after a few hours the officer exited the front door and boarded his limousine. An army truck, which had obviously been parked around the back of the house drove around to the front, the soldiers climbed on board and departed.

Geoffrey continued to wait for another hour, he hoped he wouldn't discover Zehra dead in the house. He slowly approached the door knocking three times, the door opened and Zehra stood there as beautiful as ever.

'Hello Geoffrey, I've been expecting you, please come in.'

'Hello, Zehra.'

'Would you like a cup of coffee, I expect you are feeling quite cold?'

'Yes, that would be great thank you. How come you were expecting me?'

'My brother told me, he's just left.'

'He told you I'd be back?'

'No, don't be silly, he knows nothing about you. My brother is Mustafa Kemal, he commanded the Turkish forces who beat Britain and her Allies including the Anzacs.'

'My God, I had no idea.'

'When Mustafa informed me the allies had retreated from the Gallipoli Peninsula, I figured you would return here. Geoffrey, I'm glad you did.'

'Thank you. I suppose I need to work out what I should do now, I'm half a world away from home and I have no idea where my battalion have retreated to.'

'They are in Egypt.'

'In Egypt, that's where we were stationed before we came here.'

'Mustafa has been informed they will be redeployed to France to fight the Germans.'

'How does your brother know all this?'

'He has excellent intelligence reporting to him. I suggest the best thing for you is to go back to the cottage and get good nights sleep. We can talk more about your future in the morning.'

Mustafa Ataturk
Geoffrey Becomes a Turk

Chapter 6

Geoffrey had a very restless sleep, he kept thinking about his family at home in Tasmania and how long it might be before he saw them. He also weighed up his options, if somehow he could make his way to France he could very well be court-martialled for desertion and shot. If the Turks discovered his true identity, he could be shot. The options open to him were very limited. The other disturbing thought he had was his feelings for Zehra; the time he had spent away from her made him realise his deep affection for the Turkish beauty.

Zehra also had a restless night thinking about the Australian soldier, she too had concluded that she had a deep affection for him.

The morning finally came, Zehra had invited Geoffrey to join her for breakfast. He knocked on her back door at 7 am.

'Good morning how did you sleep?'

'Not very well I'm afraid, I couldn't stop thinking about my immediate future.'

'I didn't sleep all that well either, I too was contemplating my future–with you Geoffrey.'

'What do you mean Zehra?'

'I want our futures to be together, I know it's too soon after Serkan was killed but I can't hide my feelings for you any longer.'

'I feel the same way about you, I couldn't stop thinking about you when I left here for Gallipoli.'

They both hugged and kissed each other, not letting go for what seemed an eternity.

'What are we going to do? We can't expose our relationship to anyone, at least while the war continues,' said Geoffrey.

'I agree, we must keep our relationship a close secret.'

'So what do you suggest?'

'I gave it some thought last night while lying in bed awake. The most important thing is we must never be discovered in bed together, you must always sleep in the cottage. The other important thing is for you to learn to speak and write Turkish if your future truly lies with me here in Turkey.'

'I agree on all counts, I hope I'm a good student, school and me never really got on.'

'I've known you long enough to know you're an intelligent man, you'll pick it up soon enough, after all, I'll be your tutor. You will still need to keep up the charade of being a deaf and dumb mute until this horrible war ends no matter which side wins.'

'I agree, although I can't believe it will go on much longer. Too many men are dying, including my best friend Frank. I found his grave at the cove.'

'Oh, I'm sorry to hear that.'

'I was devastated, we grew up together in Tasmania.'

Zehra put her arms around the forlorn soldier comforting him and whispering her love for him in his ear. She took his hand and led him to her bedroom. There they made love for the first time.

The relationship developed, both of them were deeply in love however they knew their love for each other must remain a secret.

Geoffrey continued to maintain the olive grove and vegetable garden, he also managed to acquire some apple seedlings, fifty in all. He planted them close to the olives.

Each night after the evening meal Zehra would tutor her lover in Turkish, her plan was to get him to the stage where he was proficient speaking the language then she would teach him the written word.

After twelve months they could have a conversation in Geoffrey's new language, his tutor was very pleased with his progress. Now it was time to learn to write. Learning the Arabic script proved to be difficult for the young Australian but with perseverance and diligence by the end of 1916 he was fluent in both the spoken and written language.

The first sentence Geoffrey wrote in Turkish was:

الزهراء أحبـــك أنـا

Translated it meant 'I love you Zehra'.

December 20, 1916

Zehra's brother Mustafa Kemal had not visited his sister for some time, she was concerned that when he did Geoffrey would be discovered and arrested.

Mustafa Kemal

She needn't have worried, her brother was busy fighting a war. He had been assigned to a new post, his adversary was the Russian army together with the Armenians. When Mustafa arrived at the front he found chaotic conditions, the region was inhospitable at the best times but with the Turkish communication lines under constant attack together with hundreds of thousands of Kurdish refugees which were hated by the Armenian units flooding over the border fleeing the advancing Russian army, Mustafa knew he had to bring some order to the petrified people while maintaining order amongst his troops.

The Russian juggernaut reached the Anatolian cities of Erzurum, Bitlis and Mus; Mustafa rallied his troops and mounted a counteroffensive. Mustafa once again demonstrated his leadership, two of his divisions captured both Bitlis and Mus. The Russian's onslaught came to a grinding halt.

Despite surrendering Mus to the Russians later in the year, through no fault of his own, he was awarded the "Golden Sword of the Order of Imtiaz" the Ottoman's highest military award.

He was given leave before taking up his new role as Commander of the Second Army he decided to visit his sister after spending time with his wife and children in Constantinople.

His Mercedes accompanied by his escort pulled up in front of the house.

Mustafa Kemal in the Back Seat

'Hello Zehra, you look wonderful. The country air continues to agree with you.'

'Thank you, Mustafa, I'm afraid I can't say the same about you, my brother, you look very tired.'

They kissed each other on both cheeks.

'Yes, I am tired–tired of fighting this war. What makes matters worse, I can't see it coming to an end anytime soon.'

'That is disturbing. I was rather hoping it would all be over by the end of this year.'

'Never mind, enough of this gloomy talk. Are you going to offer me a cup of tea?'

'Of course, I also baked a batch of your favourite biscuits, Sekepure.'

'Ah, I was hoping you would make a batch, nobody in Turkey can make Sekepure like you.'

Brother and sister sat at the kitchen table drinking their tea and eating the freshly baked biscuits when they heard a loud knock at the door. Zehra opened it, standing in front of her were two soldiers each holding the arm of her lover.

'Sir we found this man in the workers cottage. He refuses to tell us his name or what he was doing hiding in the cottage.'

'Bring him to me. Do you know this man Zehra?'

'Yes I do, he's been helping me around the farm, the reason he won't talk is because he can't, he's a deaf mute.'

'How do you communicate with him?'

'He has rudimentary writing skills, we simply write each other notes.'

'Do you know his background?'

'He was in the army under you at Gallipoli apparently, he suffered his condition fighting the invaders.'

'I see, what's his name?'

'Emir Saatchi.'

Mustafa removed a notebook from the top pocket of his uniform and a fountain pen from the other. He wrote 'What division and battalion were you assigned to?'

Emir aka Geoffrey wrote '19th Division, 3rd Battalion.'

'Who was your commander?'

'Captain Hayri.'

'His answer is correct, let him go.'

Geoffrey backed away, bowed to the General and left the house.

The siblings finished their tea and biscuits and discussed many things but not the war. After two hours Mustafa bid his sister farewell and departed back to Constantinople before joining his forces in the next stage of the war.

Once Geoffrey was convinced the Turk General had departed he re-entered the house.

'Well, we survive another day darling.'

'You did very well, lucky we rehearsed.'

'I couldn't agree more.'

'He's a very good man, I'm very proud of him.'

'I'm sure he is, he's also a bloody good soldier, he whipped us.'

'Well, at least we don't have to worry about your cover when he makes his next visit.'

'No, well I better check the apples. I'll see you for dinner.'

'OK see you soon.'

Over dinner, the lovers discussed how best to increase the returns from the farm. Even though Turkey was in the middle of a war, fresh produce was still needed to feed the general population and the troops.

'I firmly believe we can double both the olive and apple groves each year over the next five years,' Geoffrey claimed.

'That's very ambitious, do you really think we can fund that type of growth?'

'Based on our current revenue I do, it's a matter of reinvestment.'

'So how many trees would we have planted by 1922?'

'Sixteen hundred olive trees and eight hundred apple.'

'Do you have any idea of the yield?'

'We are currently getting 100 pounds of olives per tree, in another year or two we'll get 250 pounds of apples per tree.'

'Emir if we can reach those numbers the farm will be profitable.'

'That's surely our aim Zehra, we should aim for much more than self-sufficiency.'

'I'm very glad you're here with me Emir.'

'I'm very glad to be here with you.'

War Ends

Chapter 7

I destroy my enemies when I make them my friends
Abraham Lincoln.

Mustafa did not remain Commander of the Second Army for long; High Command decided he would be better utilised in the Sinai and Palestine Campaign.

His orders were to take command of the Seventh Army, soon after his appointment he returned to Istanbul where he joined Sultan Mehmed VI on a visit to Germany.

Returning to Aleppo, Syria, in late August Mustafa again took control of the seventh Army stationed in Palestine. He was under the command of the German General Liman von Sanders, the same general he reported to at Gallipoli.

Mustafa was as thorough as always visiting the frontline and talking to the troops. His assessment was that Syria was in dire straits, over 500,000 casualties, mostly attributed to famine.

The Ottomans were hated by the majority of the population and looked forward to the imminent arrival of the British. The enemy was much stronger in both troops and equipment. Mustafa knew it was only a matter of time before his troops were defeated.

Another major challenge facing Mustafa and his army was the Arab Revolt organised by the British and led by Lawrence of Arabia.

Lawrence of Arabia

The revolt was established to enable Arabs to fight against Turkish rule.

The final battle in the Middle East during the First World War was the Battle of Megiddo in September 1918.

Megiddo Ruins 7000 BCE

The ancient fortress of Megiddo appears in the New Testament as Armageddon, the location of the millennial battle between the forces of good and evil. The battle of Megiddo was the name given to the action that launched the final Allied offensive against the Turks in Palestine and Syria. Deceiving the Turkish high command that his next offensive would be launched across the Jordan River, General Sir Edmund Allenby secretly concentrated his forces on the coastal plain. His offensive began with a massed infantry assault that tore a hole in the Turkish line and allowed the mounted forces to be unleashed into the Turkish rear to sever the routes vital for supply and reinforcement. Within 24 hours the mounted troops had advanced over 50 kilometres into the Turkish rear areas. The battle of Megiddo brought about a Turkish collapse, facilitating a rapid advance on Damascus by the Allied mounted troops.

'The withdrawal ... could have been carried out in some order, if a fool like Enver Paşa had not been the director-general of the operations, if we did not have an incompetent commander–Cevat Paşa–at the head of a military force of five to ten thousand men, who fled at the first sound of gunfire, abandoned his army, and wandered around like a bewildered chicken; and the commander of the Fourth army, Cemal Paşa, ever incapable of analyzing a military situation; and if, above all, we did not have a group headquarters (under Liman von Sanders) which lost all control from the first day of the battle. Now, there is nothing left to do but to make peace.'–*Mustafa Kemal*

Mustafa Kemal was appointed to the command of Thunder Groups Command (Turkish: *Yıldırım Orduları Gurubu*), replacing Liman von Sanders. In the autumn of 1918 allied forces, having captured Jerusalem, prepared for their final lightning offensive under General Allenby on the Palestine front, in the words of an Arab historian to sweep Turks "like thistledown before the wind". Mustafa Kemal established his headquarters at Katma and succeeded in regaining control of the situation. He deployed his troops along a new defensive line at the south of Aleppo and managed to resist at the mountains. He stopped the advancing British forces (last engagements of the campaign). Kinross wrote:

Once again the Turkish hero of the campaign was Mustafa Kemal, who, after a masterly strategic retreat to the heights of Aleppo, found himself in command of the remnants of the Ottoman forces now defending the soil of Turkey itself, of which it was the natural frontier. They were still undefeated when news was received of the signature of an armistice between Britain and Turkey–leaving him, at the end of the struggle, the sole Turkish commander without a defeat to his name. Behind him were those Anatolian homelands of the Turkish race, where his future destiny and that of his people lay.—*Lord Kinross*

Mustafa Kemal's position became the baseline for the Armistice of Mudros. There were regions, such as Yemen, which was still under the Ottoman control at the time of the armistice. Kemal's last active service to the Ottoman Army was organising the return of the troops that were left behind the south of his line.

Enver was putting more hope in a German victory, but in the fall of 1918 the Germans were falling back on the Western Front in Europe, and under German generals, the Turks were falling back on the Southern Front. The British in early October seized Damascus and Beirut. The war appeared lost, and Enver and his associates stepped down from power around October 8, with Enver not staying to see what the Allies would do with him. Sultan Mehmed V had died in July, and on October 30th the Ottoman Empire, under a new Sultan Mehmed VI and a new cabinet led by Izzet Pasha, agreed to an armistice. And this left the Allies believing they were in a position to do what they pleased with the defeated Ottoman Empire.

See Epilogue for full account of Turkey post-war

Gozden irak, gonulden de irak olur.

Chapter 8

You reap what you sow
Turkish Proverb

Franklin Tasmania 1963

'What I don't understand Emir is why you didn't return home after the war ended?'

'You have to understand Paul, even though the war had ended there was still an enormous amount suspicion between the adversaries. Here I was, an Australian soldier in Turkey living with the sister of Mustafa Kemal, the commander who defeated Australia resoundingly. I was concerned that if I did return back to Australia I would be tried as a deserter; if convicted, I assumed I would be shot. I later learned no Australians were executed, but they were imprisoned.'

'Yes, I understand the predicament you were facing.'

'It wasn't just that, I was living with the women I loved in a beautiful region in Turkey with aspirations of building a sizable agricultural business. I didn't want to leave.'

'Did Zehra accompany you on this trip?'

'Sadly she died two years ago.'

'Oh, I am sorry to hear that.'

'She was a beautiful intelligent woman, she didn't deserve to die like that.'

'May I ask you how she died?'

'Cancer.'

'That's sad. Emir, do you still continue to live at Tekirdag?'

'Yes, I do, it's my home, it has been for the past 47 years.'

'And the olive and apple groves, are they still a commercial operation?'

'Very much so, Zehra and I grew the business to become the largest grower in Turkey, we decided from the beginning to produce olive oil and apple juice.'

'Wow, that sounds incredible.'

'I must admit we had some luck along the way.'

'Luck?'

'That's another story. We now export our products to over twenty countries around the world including Australia.'

'What's the company name?'

'Arilik, it translates to Purity in English.'

'I'm sorry to ask all these questions but I'm interested. My wife and I started a company ten years ago and we also have grown substantially.'

'What sort of company?'

'Transport, we started with one truck and now have a fleet of forty and growing.'

'That's impressive.'

'Ironically we probably transport your products, we deliver to Coles and Woolworths who have established new stores called supermarkets.'

'Yes, I believe we supply those two companies.'

'Emir, do you mind if I ask some more questions about your life? What happened to you and Zehra when the war finally ended?'

'The war ended in 1918 for all but Turkey it would seem, we were occupied by Britain and her allies France, Italy and Greece all eager to get a piece of what was the Ottoman Empire. The British occupied Constantinople, she was also manoeuvring to hold onto Palestine and Iraq, which they captured during the war. The Italians invaded taking Bodrum on the Aegean Sea and the French landed in Cilicia in the south of the country. The French too were intent on expanding their influence by taking Syria and Lebanon the; Ottoman Empire was no more.'

'Did the Turkish Government mount any resistance?'

'Not really, the Sultan, Mehmed VI and his ministers submitted to the authority of the Allies although some members were opposed and looked to America for help.'

'So where did this leave you and Zehra?'

'We tried to keep our heads low and continued running the orchard. It was critical that the British authorities were unaware of my true nationality.'

'Yes, I can understand your concern.'

'We also had to keep Zehra's relationship with Mustafa under wraps, he was beginning to develop an opposition movement which was proving to be a thorn in the side of the Allies. There was no love lost between Mustafa and the Sultan in Constantinople also, the war hero established a National People's Congress based in Ankara and Mustafa was elected President in April 1920.'

'I suppose the British weren't too happy about that?'

'No, they pressured the Sultan to denounce Mustafa and the NPC also Sheik-ul-Islam also denounced the movement as contrary to Islam.'

'So how did Mustafa survive all this pressure?'

'Being the military genius he was, he was able to amass a weapons cache as well as organise all the various irregulars and militia under his command. Other Turkish generals joined him bringing their troops and weapons with them.'

'How did the Turkish people respond to all of this?'

'With money and their full support, they saw Mustafa as their only hope.'

'So, it all worked out in the end?'

'Not quite, In August 1920, the Allies forced the Sultan to sign the Treaty of Sevres.'

'What was the Treaty of Sevres?'

'It limited Turkey to a military force of 50,000 men which was subject to Allied control. It also gave Britain, France and Italy control over Turkey's financial affairs as well as control over the regions they had invaded.'

'I can imagine Mustafa would have been furious.'

'What really riled him was the treaty gave the Kurds autonomy.'

'What did he do?'

'He refused to recognise the treaty.'

'What action did the Allies take to enforce the treaty?'

'The Greeks were the key in upholding the treaty or that's what the Allies thought. Mustafa's first battle as President and Supreme Leader of the Armed Services was against the Greeks. The Battle of Sakarya took place between 24 August and 16 September 1921. Mustafa Kemal and his Turkish forces won a significant victory.'

'That must have lifted morale?'

'The entire nation's morale soared.'

'The Greeks tried again in August 1922 but once again Mustafa sent them running back to Greece.'

'Is that when Mustafa became the official leader of Turkey?'

'Not quite. The Sultan now in his sixties was evacuated to Malta by the British. On November 2 the National Assembly in Ankara declared the Sultanate abolished. They also dismissed the Young Turks from the 1908 coup. The military leaders who proved to be inept during The Great War were also dismissed, including Enver Pasha.'

'Did the Allies accept the changes?'

'They did. In July 1923 in Switzerland, the Allies signed an agreement with Kemal's government that recognised Turkey's independence and its borders. It was then that Constantinople was changed to Istanbul.'

'I knew some of the histories but you've really enlightened me, Emir.'

Tekirdag Turkey 1924

'Emir, now that the war has finally ended have you thought about what you are going to do?' asked Zehra.'

'What do you mean darling?'

'Have you thought of returning to Australia?'

'I'd be lying if I told you I hadn't given it some thought, but no I have no

64

intention of returning. I regard Turkey as my home now besides I could never leave you.'

'Then I think we should get married.'

'My God, yes, I'd love to marry you.'

'There is one thing stopping us.'

'What's that?'

'To marry me you need to convert to Islam.'

'Fine, where do I sign?'

'It's quite easy, you simply need to say 'I testify "La ihaha illa Allah, Mulu Allah, Muhammad rasoolu Allah.'

'Really? All I have to say is "there is no true God but Allah and Muhammad is the messenger of God"?'

'That's all, but you must say it with conviction.'

'Do I have to visit a mosque to say it?'

'No, you can say it to me.'

Once the conversion had been completed Zehra raised another issue.

'We also need to tell my brother about us, the complete story. If he refuses his blessing we will not be able to be married.'

'Yes, I thought I would have to face him eventually.'

'I will invite him down from Ankara, hopefully he will be able to come soon, after all, he has many responsibilities these days.'

Mustafa committed to visiting his sister the following month along with his entourage and military guards.

Where there is love there is life.

Mahatma Gandhi

Chapter 9

June 1924

The Presidential convoy could be seen a mile from the homestead winding its way up the dirt road, leaving a cloud of dust in its wake. The convoy consisted of four army trucks and two limousines; the vehicle in the middle contained Mustafa and two security officers, the vehicle behind contained army officers. Once the convoy reached the house all but Mustafa's car parked behind the building, Mustafa's vehicle parked directly outside the front door.

The new Turkish president greeted his sister at the door.

'Hello, Mr President.'

'Hello, my dear sister; how are you?'

'I'm well, please come inside.'

Mustafa entered the house while the two security officers remained outside, one each side of the entrance.

Once inside he hugged his sister and kissed her on both cheeks.

'Now, that you are the president do you prefer to have your coffee in the dining room?'

'I think you're being sarcastic little sister; I'm happy to be entertained in the kitchen as usual thank you.'

'No doubt you expected me to bake some sekepure?'

'I would be very disappointed if you didn't.'

'Of course, I did, last time you were here you ate five!'

'Oh, I see you were counting.'

'Not really.'

Brother and sister sat at the kitchen table drinking their coffee and eating the freshly baked Turkish biscuits. After thirty minutes or, so Zehra brought up the subject of Emir.

'Mustafa I've met a man whom I wish to marry.'

'Really, well I think its time you got on with your life, although I'm a little surprised you've never mentioned him before. Who is he? Where did you meet him?'

'His name is Emir and I met him in the barn.'

'I think you need to explain Zehra.'

She recounted the whole story in every detail monitoring her brother's reaction as she told her tale.

'I'd like to meet him, however by the sounds of it I've met him before.'

Zehra departed from the room and entered Emir's cottage he was feeling extremely nervous.

'Have you told him yet?'

'I have, he wants to meet you.'

'How did he react?'

'I don't know, he's never been one to show his feelings.'

'Maybe we should wait.'

'Don't be foolish Emir, now come on he's waiting.'

The two lovers walked slowly back to the house and entered the kitchen. Mustafa remained seated at the table.

'So, I believe you are an Australian?'

'That's right Sir.'

'You deserted in the Gallipoli campaign?'

'No Sir, that's incorrect. I was on a reconnaissance mission to determine Turkish strength prior to us attacking your position at the Nek. I was captured by your troops.'

'I wish you'd been successful in your mission then maybe your commanders would have abandoned the attack. It was a bloody slaughter.'

'So I understand.'

Emir, answered all the president's questions. When the interview had been completed Mustafa was satisfied with the truth of the story.

'You are asking permission to marry my sister, yet you are a non-Muslim.'

'Sir, I have converted to the Islamic faith.'

'When?'

'One month ago.'

'I can see Zehra is very much in love with you Emir, and it's obvious you are with her. I give you my permission to wed.'

'Thank you, sir, I promise I will look after her for the rest of her life.'

'Well, if you don't you'll have me to answer to.'

Zehra hugged her brother while Emir shook his hand. The mood had changed, instead of the tenseness of the previous hour everybody was happy and looking forward to the future.

'One issue I see is the fact Emir is an Australian. We need to address this problem,' said Mustafa.

'What can we do?' asked Zehra.

'I will arrange for a birth certificate to be produced. What's your date of birth Emir?'

'January 1, 1893.'

'And where in Turkey would you like to have been born?'

'Bodrum.'

'OK, I'll arrange your birth certificate to be sent to you before the wedding ceremony.'

Mustafa and his entourage departed for Ankara; Zehra and Emir had a wedding to arrange. It was decided it would be held in Tekirdag at the Rustem Pasa Mosque instead of the Blue Mosque in Istanbul which would normally be expected for the wedding of the president's sister. The couple and Mustafa wished to keep it as low-key as possible.

Rustem Pasa Mosque

The date for the wedding was set for December 20, 1925 Zehra invited her extended family excluding her father who had died several years before. Emir had no friends or family to invite.

Zehra took part in the Henna party the day before the wedding—cousins and friends applied the dye to her hands then sang and danced and generally had a good time. While the party was taking place Emir was at home reading a book about diamonds.

The wedding was a typical Islamic affair enjoyed by the bride and groom and their guests. Geoffrey aka Emir couldn't help thinking about his family back in Tasmania but there was nothing he could do. Zehra and Emir enjoyed a one-week honeymoon in Bodrum a beautiful ancient city on the Aegean Sea.

Bodrum Turkey

The couple's plan was to return to Tekirdag and complete the olive tree orchard expansion they had been working on before the wedding. Their objective was to plant another 100 trees bringing the total up to 350.

January 1, 1925

Emir had completed his work for the day. He had planted 20 trees, a solid day's work on his 31st birthday. He entered the kitchen where Zehra was preparing their evening meal and placed a dirty cloth bag on the table. He opened up the parcel displaying a bunch of small rocks and stones.

'Emir take those of the table I was about to set it.'

'I'm sorry darling, but I wanted to show you these; I think you will be interested.'

'Why would I be interested in some dirty old rocks?'

'Because they're diamonds.'

'Don't be ridiculous.'

'You'll see once I wash them in the sink.'

Emir took the parcel of stones, filled the sink with warm soapy water and scrubbed them rigorously, laying them out on a tea towel on the kitchen bench.

'Now come and have a look at them now they're clean.'

'They just look glass to me, how can you tell if they're real diamonds?'

Emir grabbed one of the larger stones and walked to the kitchen window where he scratched a deep mark on the glass.

'There that proves it is a diamond.'

'Where did you find them?'

'When I was digging holes for the olive trees. I didn't realise what they were at first, but one glinted at me in the sun. I bought a book on diamonds and read up on them'

'When?'

'A while ago before the wedding.'

'You knew about them then?'

'I still wasn't sure, I thought it better to wait until there wasn't a doubt.'

'Emir have you got any idea how many diamonds there might be under the orchard?'

'No, not until we start excavating.'

'Do you really want to live next door to a diamond mine?'

'No, I don't, but I'm sure we can keep it secret. It doesn't have to be a huge operation.'

'My uncle is the largest jeweller in Istanbul, I think we should get him to asses them.'

'Yes, I think that's a good idea although we shouldn't divulge where they came from or we'll have fortune hunters crawling all over the place.'

Zehra telephoned her uncle and arranged for Emir and herself to meet with the jeweller the following Monday. He owned several jewellery stores in the Grand Bazaar known for its gold and diamonds.

The expectant couple drove to Istanbul, the journey took them four hours in their Ford Model T Pickup.

Emir parked the pickup close to the Grand Bazaar, he and Zehra walked the two hundred yards to the market. The Bazaar was alive with people, both shoppers and shop owners milling about bargaining or simply window shopping.

Zehra's uncle, Ahmet had his store, "Elmas" in the heart of the jewellery section, it stood out by its size compared to the other shops close by.

The young couple entered the store. Ahmet noticed them immediately and waved them through to the back of the shop.

Emir had met Zehra's uncle at their wedding so the greetings were warm and friendly.

'So what is it I can do for you? Possibly a new ring for Zehra or maybe a bracelet?'

'We're not here to purchase jewellery Uncle Ahmet, we're here to get your advice.'

'I see and what advice to you seek?'

Emir withdrew a velvet pouch from his coat and spread the uncut diamonds onto the brass table in front of them.

'Praise Allah where did you get these?'

'We can't tell you at the moment but we can assure you they are legally ours,' said Zehra.

'May I examine them?'

'Please do.'

The excited jeweller took a loupe from his pocket, attached it to his right eye and began examining each stone, twenty in all. Most of the diamonds varied in size. Ahmet took thirty minutes to examine the stones in complete silence. Zehra and Emir looked on anxiously. Finally, Ahmet extracted the loupe from his eye sitting back in his chair he looked at the expectant couple.

'Well, this is quite extraordinary; I must say I haven't seen so many high-grade stones in one collection before. Normally one or two stones stand out and the remainder are quite ordinary but all these stones are of the highest quality.'

'So I take it they're saleable?' asked Emir.

'When they are cut, yes very much so.'

'Can you cut them?'

'No, not me, however, I know a very skilled diamond cutter here in Istanbul.'

'Could we ask you to arrange the cutting for us?'

'I could, but I need to know where they came from. I know you say they are legally yours but I need proof.'

'Would you mind if we went a got a coffee and talked about it?'

'No, not all Zehra take your time. Do you want to take the diamonds?'

'No, you keep them here uncle, I don't fancy walking around the Bazaar with them in my handbag.'

The couple left the jewellery store and walked through the bazaar looking for a suitable coffee shop.

Grand Bazaar

They found a suitable cafe and ordered two coffees.

'So, what do you think, should we tell him about the olive grove? asked Emir.

'He's my uncle, I trust him, but we need to have a written agreement prohibiting him from divulging the location,' said Zehra.

'I agree, we also need to have included in the agreement costs for cutting and his commission for selling the finished diamonds.'

They walked back to "Elmas". Ahmet greeted them once again and the three of them retreated to the back of the shop.

'So have you made your decision?'

'Yes, uncle we have.'

Zehra and Emir explained how and where they found the stones. They also elucidated their concern relating to developing a full-scale mine.

'I understand completely I'm happy to sign an agreement as well as give you my word. While you were having coffee I calculated the stones worth, I assume you'd be interested?'

'Yes, we would, naturally,' said Zehra

'Once they are cut and polished I estimate their worth to be 60,000 Lire.'

'Praise Allah, are you sure?'

'I'm very sure. These are E grade diamonds, only D are higher and they are very rare.'

'Well, we authorise you to get the stones cut as soon as the paperwork is arranged,' said Zehra.

'Certainly, we also need to agree to my commission for the sale.'

'Absolutely, how much do you normally charge?'

'Twenty-five percent, but considering you are family I'll make it twenty.'

'Thank you, uncle, that seems very fair'

'The cutting and polishing of the twenty stones would be about 6,000 Lire.'

Zehra and Emir did a quick mental calculation; they would net 42,000 Lire, a small fortune, with possibly much more to come from the olive grove.

'I'll write up an agreement and post it to you, Uncle Ahmet. Once you sign it we will be ready to proceed.'

Zehra kissed her uncle, Emir shook his hand and they departed both feeling euphoric. The trip back was taken up with discussions on how best to invest their windfall. By the time they reached their home they had decided the bulk of the money should be used in expanding their agricultural enterprise including purchasing additional land. This became the genesis of "Arilik"

While Zehra and Emir were busy building their business Mustafa was busy building the new republic.

Father of Modern Day Turkey

Chapter 10

Mustafa knew if Turkey was to survive it had to throw off the ancient shackles of the Ottoman Empire and become a modern country, a republic.

He did this by transforming:

Legal System

'We must liberate our concepts of justice, our laws and legal institutions from the bonds which hold a tight grip on us although they are incompatible with the needs of our century.'

Between 1926 and 1930, the Turkish Republic achieved a legal transformation, which might have required decades in most other countries. Sharia law was abolished, and a secular system of jurisprudence introduced. The concepts, the texts and contexts of the laws were made harmonious with the progressive thrust of Mustafa's Turkey. *'The nation has placed its faith in the precept that all laws should be inspired by actual needs here on earth as a basic fact of national life.'*

Among the far-reaching changes were the new Civil Code, Penal Code, and Business Law, based on the Swiss, Italian and German models respectively.

The new legal system made all citizens - men and women, rich and poor - equal before the law. It gave Turkey a firm foundation for a society of justice and equal rights.

Social Reforms

'The major challenge facing us is to elevate our national life to the highest level of civilisation and prosperity.'

Mustafa's ambition was to modernise Turkish life in order to give his nation a new sense of dignity, equality, and happiness. After more than three centuries of high achievement, the Ottoman Empire had declined from the 17th to the early

20th Century: With Sultans presiding over a social and economic system mired in backwardness, the Ottoman state had become hopelessly outmoded for the modern times. Mustafa resolved to lead his country out of the ancient past into a brave new future.

In his program of modernization, secular government and education played a major role. He made religious faith a matter of individual conscience; he created a truly secular system in Turkey, where the vast Moslem majority and the small Christian and Jewish minorities were free to practice their faith. As a result of Mustafa's reforms, Turkey, unlike scores of other countries, had fully secular institutions.

The leader of modern Turkey aspired to freedom and equality for all. When he proclaimed the Republic, he announced, *'The new Turkish State is a state of the people and a state by the people.'* Having established a populist and egalitarian system, Mustafa later observed: *'We are a nation without classes or special privileges.'* He also highlighted the importance of the peasant class, who had long been neglected in the Ottoman times: *'The true owner and master of Turkey is the peasant who is the real producer.'*

Mustafa introduced many reforms: European hats replaced the fez; women stopped wearing the veil; all citizens took surnames, and the Islamic calendar gave way to the Western calendar. A vast transformation took place in both urban and rural life. It can be said that few nations have ever experienced anything comparable to the social change in Mustafa Atatürk's Turkey.

Economic Growth

'In order to raise our new Turkey to the level that she is worthy of, we must, under all circumstances, attach the highest importance to the national economy.'

When the Turkish Republic was established in 1923, it lacked capital, industry, and expertise. Successive wars had decimated manpower, agricultural production stood at an all-time low, and the huge foreign debts of the defunct Ottoman state confronted the new Republic.

President Atatürk swiftly moved to initiate a dynamic program of economic development. *'Our nation has crushed the enemy forces. But to achieve independence we must observe the following rule: National sovereignty should be supported by financial independence. The only power that will propel us to this goal is the economy. No matter how mighty they are, political and military victories cannot endure unless they are crowned by economic triumphs.'*

With determination and vigour, Atatürk's Turkey undertook agricultural expansion, industrial growth, and technological advancement. In mining, transportation, manufacturing, banking, exports, social services, housing, communications, energy, mechanisation, and other vital areas, many goals were achieved. Within the decade, the gross national product increased five-fold.

Turkey's economic development during Atatürk's Presidency was impressive in absolute figures and in comparison to other countries. The synthesis that evolved at that time -state enterprises and private initiative active in both industrial and agricultural growth serves as the basis of the economic structure not only for Turkey but also in dozen countries.

New Language

'The cornerstone of education is an easy system of reading and writing. The key to this is the new Turkish alphabet based on the Latin script.'

One of the most difficult changes to achieve in any society is language reform. Most nations never attempt it; those who do, usually prefer a gradual approach. Under Mustafa's Leadership, Turkey undertook the modern world's swiftest and most extensive language reform. In 1928, he decided that the Arabic script, which had been used for a thousand years, should be replaced with the Latin alphabet.

His advisors suggested it would take five years to transform the language, Mustafa gave them six months.

As the 1920s came to an end, Turkey had converted to the European model. The language reform enabled children and adults to read and write more quickly and to study Western languages with greater effectiveness.

Mustafa Atatürk's language reform encompassing the script, grammar, and vocabulary stands as one of the most far-reaching in history. It overhauled Turkish culture and education.

Women's Rights

'Everything we see in the world is the creative work of women.'

With total faith in the vital importance of women in society, Mustafa Atatürk launched many reforms to give Turkish women equal rights and opportunities. The new Civil Code, adopted in 1926, abolished polygamy and recognised the equal rights of women in divorce, custody, and inheritance. The entire educational system from the grade school to the university became co-educational. Atatürk greatly admired the support that the national liberation struggle received from women and praised their many contributions: *'In Turkish society, women have not lagged behind men in science, scholarship, and culture. Perhaps they have even gone further ahead.'* He gave women the same opportunities as men, including full political rights. In the mid-1930s, 18 women, among them a villager, were elected to the national parliament. Later, Turkey had the world's first women Supreme Court Justice.

Education

'The government's most creative and significant duty is education.'

Atatürk regarded education as the force that would galvanise the nation. After the War of Independence, he made it known he wished to serve as Minister of Education. As President of the Republic, he spared no effort to stimulate and expand education at all levels and for all segments of the society.

Turkey initiated a most ambitious program of schooling for children and adults. From grade school to graduate school, education was made free, secular, and co-educational. Primary education was declared compulsory. The armed forces implemented an extensive program of literacy. Atatürk heralded *"The Army of Enlightenment"*. Literacy increased from 9 percent in 1923 to more than 33 percent by 1938.

Women's education was very close to Atatürk's heart. In 1922, even before proclaiming the Republic, he vowed: *'We shall emphasise putting our women's secondary and higher education on an equal footing with men.'*

To give impetus to science and scholarship, Atatürk transformed the University of Istanbul (founded in the mid-15th century) into a modern university in 1933. A few years later, the University of Ankara became into being.

Culture and the Arts

'We shall make the expansion and rise of Turkish culture in every era the mainstay of the Republic.'

Atatürk stated: *'Culture is the foundation of the Turkish Republic.'* His view of culture encompassed the nation's creative legacy as well as the best values of world civilisation. He stressed personal and universal humanism. *'Culture is a basic element in being a person worthy of humanity.'*

To create the best synthesis, Atatürk underlined the need for the utilisation of all the viable elements in the national heritage, including the ancient indigenous cultures, and the arts and techniques of the entire world civilisation, past and present. He gave impetus to the study of the earlier civilisations of Anatolia— including Hittite, Phrygian, Lydian, and others. Pre-Islamic culture of the Turks became the subject of extensive research, which proved that, long before their Seljuk and Ottoman Empires, the Turks had already created a civilisation of their own. Atatürk also stressed the folk arts of the countryside as the wellspring of Turkish creativity.

Peace

'Mankind is a single body and each nation a part of that body. We must never say 'What does it matter to me if some part of the world is ailing?' If there is such an illness, we must concern ourselves with it as though we were having that illness.'

A military hero who had won significant victories including Gallipoli, Atatürk knew the value of peace and, during his presidency, did his utmost to secure and strengthen it throughout the world. Few of the world leaders in modern times spoke with Atatürk's eloquence on the need to create a world order based on peace, on the dignity of all human beings, and on the constructive interdependence of all nations. He stated, immediately after the Turkish War of Independence, *'Peace is the most effective way for nations to attain prosperity and happiness.'* Later as he concluded treaties of friendship and created regional ententes, he affirmed: *'Turks are the friends of all civilised nations.'* The new Turkey established cordial relations with all countries, including those powers, which years earlier had been at war with Turkey. The new republic did not pursue a policy of expansionism, and never engaged in any act contrary to peaceful co-existence. Atatürk signed pacts with Greece, Rumania and Yugoslavia in the Balkans, and with Iran, Iraq and Afghanistan in the East. He maintained friendly relations with the Soviet Union, the United States, England, Germany, Italy, and France. In the early 1930s, he and the Greek Premier Venizelos initiated and signed a treaty of peace and cooperation.

The Armenian genocide has long been a blot on Turkey's humanitarian record.

In an interview Mustafa Kemal Ataturk gave to the *Los Angeles Examiner* newspaper published on 1 August 1926 he stated:

"The second element, I am now about to deal with ruthlessly, is the group of men who in the pre-republic days were known to the world as the Committee of the Union of the Young Turks.

I am about to show these plotters that the Republic of Turkey cannot be overthrown by murderers or through their murderous designs.

These leftovers from the former Young Turkey Party, who should have been made to account for the lives of millions of our Christian subjects who were ruthlessly driven en masse from their homes and massacred, have been restive under the Republican rule. They have hitherto lived on plunder, robbery and bribery and become inimical to any idea or suggestion to enlist in useful labour and earn their living by the honest sweat of their brow."–*Mustafa Kemal Atatürk*

His creation of modern Turkey and his contribution to the world have made Atatürk an historic figure of enduring influence.

The Building of an Empire

"Arilik"

Chapter 11

1929

Zehra and Emir decided to approach the landowner next to their orchard to see if he would sell them a portion of his land. They were hoping to purchase fifty acres. Sitting at the kitchen table they discussed their plans.

'If Mohammad agrees to the sale would you plant both apples and olives on the land?' Zehra asked.

'My initial feeling is that the ground it a little too rocky for apples, I think we would be better off planting olives.'

'Do you think there could be diamonds on the plot?'

'There could be, the seam on our land tends to run in his direction. He obviously doesn't suspect there would be diamonds, after all he only runs a few goats on the property.'

'So, when do you plan to approach him?'

'I thought I'd wander over tomorrow morning.'

'So, we agree we'll offer him 20,000 Lire and go to 25,000 if we need to?'

'Yes, that's the plan.'

The next morning at 10 am Emir approached the house of Mohammad, he found him sitting on his front veranda sipping coffee.

'Good morning neighbour, how are you on this beautiful morning?'

'Hello Emir, would you like to join me?'

'I'd like to, thank you.'

Muhammad entered the modest house and poured a coffee from the old beaten coffee percolator which had been sitting on the wood stove in the kitchen. The two men sat on the veranda sipping their strong coffee talking about the weather and other innocuous subjects. Finally Emir brought up the topic of buying the land.

'How much are you willing to pay me, Emir?'

'How much do you want Muhammad?'

'I don't know, if I decided to sell I'd want 30,000 Lire.'

'Goodness me, I'm sorry, I couldn't pay you that much.'

'What would you be prepared to pay for it?'

'I was thinking 20,000.'

'Make it 25,000 and it's yours.'

The two men shook hands, the deal had been done. All that was needed was a new title and the transfer of the funds.

The following month the transaction was finalised. The first task that needed to be completed was to erect fencing so the goats couldn't eat the young olive trees when they were planted. Their goal for the future was to plant 100 trees on 10 acres and increase the orchard each six months by a further 100 trees until they planted out the full 50 acres with 500 olive trees. Once they completed the planting the orchard combined with the original would have 2100 trees, a projected harvest of 210,000 pounds of olives a year.

Emir continued to find diamonds throughout the orchard, every second or third hole they dug more stones were discovered. He hadn't begun the planting in the new orchard as yet he didn't see the urgency, by the time the additional trees had been planted in the original orchard they had amassed 200 diamonds.

'Emir, when do you think we should visit Uncle Ahmet again?'

'I was only thinking about it this afternoon, what with the purchase of the land and the additional trees we purchased from the nursery we're going to need more capital. I was also contemplating purchasing additional land to increase the apple harvest if you were in agreement'

'I agree, we've been concentrating on the olives and neglecting the apple crop.'

'Why don't you telephone Uncle Ahmet and arrange for a meeting?'

'I will, how many diamonds will I say we'll be bringing?'

'I don't think we should take the entire parcel, it could arouse suspicion from other jewellers. I suggest we take half, 100 stones.'

'OK, that sounds reasonable, I'll call him.'

Zehra called her uncle, they agreed the following Tuesday would suit both parties.

They began their journey to Istanbul, departing at 5 am, arriving at 9 am, opening time for the Grand Bazaar. Ahmet was in the shop waiting for them. After the normal greeting they retired to the rear of the premises.

Emir spread the diamonds on the brass table explaining there were 100 in total. The jeweller attached his loupe to his right eye and began examining the small treasure. As he did he made noises that indicated his pleasure re the quality of the diamonds. After an hour, he returned the loupe into his pocket and looked at the expectant couple.

'You've done it again, I estimate 80 stones are D quality.'

'Excellent, and the remaining 20?'

'F, not as good but still of high quality.'

'So, what would our net be uncle?'

'After cutting and my commission I'd say between 200,000 and 220,000 Lire, depending on the market.'

'We'd be happy with that,' said Zehra.

'I'll arrange for the funds to be available to you by the end of the week.'

Zehra and Emir used the money to purchase more land close to their original orchard. By 1931 they had acquired an additional 1000 acres and employed a workforce of over 100 people including a management group of five.

Each orchard, once productive, had either an apple press or an olive press depending on the crop the bottling plant was located on the original orchard now named "Utopia".

1935

ARILIK had become the largest and most profitable agricultural business in Turkey. As well as olives and apples they invested in producing dairy products and raising beef cattle.

March 1935

Zehra and Emir received an invitation from Mustafa Kemal Ataturk to attend a state dinner to welcome the German Ambassador to Turkey, Mr Hans Kroll. The couple would receive one or two invitations a year, it gave Zehra a chance to catch up with her brother as well as Emir who had established a strong bond with his brother in law.

The couple were allocated a spacious guest wing in the Presidential Mansion, they didn't want for anything.

"Cankaya" Presidential Mansion, Ankara

Zehra and Emir settled into their luxurious suite. In the mid afternoon a knock came about 4 pm, it was one of the presidential butlers with a message for them to join Mustafa in his quarters.

The butler escorted the couple to the rear of the mansion where Mustafa's apartment enjoyed a view of the extensive gardens.

Having announced the visitors the butler retreated and the three family members greeted each other with the usual warmth.

'It's good to see you both, thank you for coming. Can I interest you in a glass of Raki?'

'Thank you, Mustafa, I'll have one. How about you, Emir?'

'I've been a Turk for over twenty years now and I still can't tolerate the taste, too much aniseed for me, it reminds me of Ouzo. May I ask you for a cold beer Mustafa?'

'Of course you can Emir, just like you do every time you visit. There's a reason why I invited you here on this particular occasion, I would like your opinion of our guest of honour Hans Kroll.'

'Why are you asking us brother?'

'As you are aware Hitler is building up Germany's military might, I'm sure he is going to look to Turkey to become part of the Axis.'

'Are you considering agreeing to his request?'

'He hasn't come to me yet, it's just my strong premonition.'

'Would you consider it if he did?'

'No, I have no intention of leading Turkey into another disastrous war. Turkey will remain neutral. That's not to say we won't sell our goods to Germany nor Britain or France or whoever gets pulled into another world war for that matter.'

'So, what in particular do you want us to assess while speaking with Ambassador Kroll?'

'I'd Just like your general opinion, you know things like do you think he's trustworthy.'

'OK, we'll do our best,' said Emir.

Hans Kroll

Diplomacy

Chapter 12

War is failure of diplomacy.
John Dingell

Reception at the Presidential Mansion

The time was 7 pm, cars carrying the guests were beginning to arrive parking under the grand portico. The passengers were alighting from the limousines and being welcomed by the Turkish President Mustafa Kemal Ataturk. Diplomats and their spouses from England, America, France, Spain, and many more countries who maintained diplomatic relations with Turkey including Australia were present.

The distinguished guests were ushered into the grand ballroom where drinks and canapés were being served prior to the dinner in the grand dining room.

Emir and Zehra did not find the opportunity to converse with the German ambassador, however this was of little consequence as Mustafa had arranged that they sit next to Hans Kroll at dinner.

Two tables each capable of seating forty guests were arranged parallel to each other, each chair had a place name so the waiters could easily ensure each guest sat in his or her allocated place at the table.

The German ambassador and his wife were seated next to Zehra and Emir on one side and Mustafa Ataturk and his partner on the other.

The entrée Meze, comprised of various Turkish dishes including olives picked from the trees of Arilik.

'Mr Ambassador, may I ask you how you are enjoying living in Turkey?'

'Very much Madam Saatchi, I have seen quite a lot but I believe there is much more to be discovered.'

'What particularly interests you about my country?'

'The ancient sites. I have a strong interest in archaeology.'

'Emir and I share your fascination, we have been involved in several digs.'

'Oh, where have you dug?'

'Gobeklitepe would be the most significant.'

'Ah, that's definitely on my list.'

'If you don't mind me asking, do you think the world is heading for another world war?'

'I sincerely hope not but that does depend on much of Europe.'

'What do you mean?'

'After the First World War Germany was penalised harshly, our economy had no chance of recovering. The Versailles Agreement became a huge millstone around Germany's neck. Hitler has begun the reconstruction of Germany, she will have a strong economy and the people will regain their pride. Hitler does not want war, he is a man of peace.'

'So how can Europe ensure a lasting peace?'

'By allowing Germany to rebuild totally, the Fuhrer has built magnificent stadiums and other sporting facilities for the Olympic games next year. He has also begun the task of rebuilding the military. Hitler has ordered Hermann Goering to establish the Luftwaffe, the German air force, in defiance of the terms of the Treaty of Versailles. A strong Germany means world peace.'

'I hope you're right Mr Ambassador'

'Did you know the Fuhrer idolises your brother? He holds him on a pedestal, a very high pedestal.'

'No, I didn't know that, but then again many people admire Mustafa for what he's done for Turkey.'

'Exactly. The Fuhrer believes we must follow his model in rebuilding Germany.'

The main course was served giving Zehra some respite from the enthusiastic ambassador. Ironically the Australian Ambassador, James Hall, was seated next to Emir.

'Well, Emir I believe you are the President's brother in law?'

'That's correct Mr Ambassador.'

'Please don't be so formal, call me Jim. Have you ever been to Australia Emir?'

'I'm afraid not, however, I'd like to visit one day. My wife and I have a sizable agricultural company and Australia is seen as a world leader in agriculture.'

'Really what do you grow?'

'We started with olives and apples and have since diversified into dairy and beef cattle.'

'I come from Tasmania, we're known for our apples. We export most of our crop to the United Kingdom.'

'As if I didn't know that,' thought Emir.

The evening concluded and the guests began to leave, the line of diplomatic limousines stretched the length of the driveway. When Mustafa had farewelled the last of the guests he invited Zehra and Emir back to his apartment.

'Can I interest you two in a nightcap?'

'Yes, thank you, Mustafa I'll have a port,' said Zehra.

'What about you Emir?'

'I'll have a glass of beer thank you.'

Mustafa ordered his butler to get the drinks including a glass of Raki for himself.

'Well, what did you think of Hans Kroll?'

'I think he's a very committed Nazi,' said Zehra.

'Do you think we can trust him? Will he be supportive of Turkey?'

'Only if it is in his own interest and that of his beloved Fuhrer. I have little doubt that Germany is heading towards a global war.'

'Yes, I think you're right sister. What about you Emir what are your thoughts?'

'I didn't get to talk with him all that much but the conversations I did have would lead me to support Zehra's view.'

'I'm about to ask you something Zehra, and I want you to know you are under no obligation to agree to my request.'

'My goodness, that sounds ominous Mustafa. Go ahead and ask me.'

'I need someone I can trust who has the intelligence and diplomatic skills to become ambassador to Germany for the next three years. I'd like that person to be you. I also believe having Emir by your side would be wonderful support.'

'I can't believe what I'm hearing Mustafa, I have no experience in the diplomatic corps. I'm not sure I could live up to your high expectations.'

'Trust me, I know you would make an excellent ambassador. I need you to be in Germany, Turkey needs you to be in Germany.'

'Mustafa, you will have to give Emir and I time to discuss it. There are many things to consider, including the business.'

'I understand, I didn't expect an answer immediately. What I will say is the Government will provide you with the resources needed to ensure Arilik continues to operate profitably while you are away.'

'When would you like an answer?'

'There's no rush, take your time to consider my proposal thoroughly.'

Zehra and Emir bid Mustafa good night retiring to the guest wing. Neither of them slept well that night.

Utopia, Tekirdag, April 1935

Zehra and Emir were sitting at the kitchen table, the same table that had witnessed so many events and decisions made in their lives to date.

'What are your thoughts darling, now that we've had some time to think about it?' asked Zehra.

'I have mixed feelings, part of me believes this would be a wonderful opportunity to pay back Turkey for all that she has provided us. The other part, the practical part, tells me we have a large profitable company that requires both our input on a daily basis.'

'We do have a very strong management team and Mustafa did say he would provide support if we needed it.'

'Maybe we should ask him what sort of support he would be willing to offer.'

'I'm not worried about the orchards so much, it's the dairy and beef cattle that is giving me concern.'

'Yes, I do understand they will need constant monitoring.'

Mustafa organised two cattle experts one dairy the other beef to visit Zehra and Emir at Utopia on the basis they would be available to the couple while they were away in Germany.

Beren and Karem arrived on Friday 7 August. After the introductions were completed Emir arranged for the two experts to tour the dairy farm where 400 dairy cattle produced over a million litres of milk per year. This was regarded as an excellent yield.

The party then drove 100 miles to the beef cattle ranch where 2000 cattle were grazed on 5000 acres.

Beren and Karem were impressed with the Arilik operation. They had no doubt with their help the agricultural business would operate as normal if the owners decided to take up the German assignment.

The two men returned to Utopia with Emir to discuss their findings with Zehra and determine if she felt comfortable with them overseeing the business while they were in Germany. Emir had already made it clear that he was satisfied and would have no problem leaving the business under their management.

The decision was made that night at the kitchen table, they would agree to Mustafa's request, Zehra would become the first women in Turkish history to be appointed the ambassador to a foreign country.

She telephoned her brother and informed him of their decision. Mustafa was delighted, he suggested a visit to Ankara the following week to initiate the process of briefings.

Mustafa arranged for a Government limousine to collect the couple and bring them to Ankara where they stayed in the presidential mansion, their usual accommodation when visiting Mustafa.

The president welcomed his sister and brother-in-law, inviting them to his private apartment for their first drink of the day and his sixth.

'Welcome Madam Ambassador, can I offer you a Raki?'

'Yes thank you, Mr President.'

'I won't bother asking you Emir, no doubt you would like a cold beer.'

'Thank you, Mustafa.'

Mustafa rang through the order to his butler, five minutes later their drinks were served from a silver tray. Emir was astounded when handed his glass of beer.

'Mustafa how on earth did you find a bottle of Fosters?'

'I'm the President Emir, I can get anything I want. By the way, I ordered six dozen which will be waiting for you at the Turkish embassy in Berlin.'

'Thank you, Mustafa, I've dreamed of enjoying an ice cold Fosters since I arrived in Turkey.'

'So, everybody's happy. Tomorrow you meet with Mr Aidan Baydar the retiring ambassador, he will brief you on what's happening in Germany at the moment and who you need to meet and who you need to watch out for. First on the list is Hitler.'

The following morning Zehra and Emir joined the ambassador for breakfast in the conservatory overlooking the gardens. The day was perfect with blue sky and a gentle breeze. Zehra inquired about Hitler.

'What was he like, Aidan? Intimidating? Or comical?'

'Certainly not comical, the first time I met him I arrived at Bismarck's former palace where Hitler has his quarters. It was quite daunting, climbing up a very wide set of marble stairs guarded at every landing and turn by a Nazi SS soldier with their hands raised in Roman style.'

'Did you feel compelled to return the Hitler salute, Ambassador?' asked Emir.

'I just bowed my head slightly. I certainly wasn't going to comply with their ridiculous laws regarding salutations. I waited in his ante-room until the Minister for Foreign Affairs von Neurath invited me into the Chancellor's office, a room some fifty feet square with tables and chairs scattered about for group conferences.'

'Did you feel nervous at all?' Zehra inquired.

'No, Zehra, not really, I sat there in great anticipation, not knowing really what to expect.'

'I suppose he looked quite impressive in his Nazi uniform.'

'Actually I was quite surprised, he had dressed in a simple lounge suit, neat and erect-looking. Better in person than he had appeared in newspaper photos I had seen.'

'Aidan, are you permitted to divulge what you discussed with him?' asked Emir.

'It wasn't particularly confidential Emir. I raised the assaults upon Turks and the discriminations against Turkish Jews. He seemed very concerned. The German dictator even assured me that future attacks against Turkish citizens in Nazi Germany would be strictly punished and that he would issue decrees that foreigners were not obliged to offer the Nazi salute.'

'So you had a win in your first meeting with 'the great man'!'

'Well, not entirely. The conversation turned to Nazi Germany's withdrawal the previous Saturday from the League of Nations. I called it a 'thunderbolt', totally unexpected. This really started him off. He ranted about the Treaty of Versailles, the failure of the powers to keep their promises about disarmament and the indignity of keeping Germany in a defenceless status. We discussed various other matters, which I am not at liberty to divulge. No doubt when your appointment has been made official you will be fully briefed. I departed after about forty-five minutes.'

'What was your overall impression of Hitler, Aidan?'

'He's certainly a man not to be taken lightly.'

'Well I'm sure it is a meeting you will never forget,' said Emir.

They concluded their breakfast and went their separate ways. Zehra and Emir dined with the president that night and returned to Utopia the following morning. It was agreed that Zehra and Emir would commence their tenure in Berlin on December 12 1935.

Berlin

The Ambassador greeted the two new appointees at the Turkish embassy located in Mitte, Tiergartenstrabe in central Berlin. They were both keen to receive a comprehensive briefing from Aidan Baydar prior to his recall to Ankara. Ambassador Baydar's final assessment of Hitler and his regime was as follows:

'Let's begin with my assessment of Hitler's political past and future. I should go back a couple of years so you can appreciate where he has come from and where he's heading.

'Hitler's political movement, which was practically down and out following the abortive *putsch* in Munich in 1923, gained a large ascendency with the increase of unemployment in Germany. The Nazi Party witnessed phenomenal gains in successive local elections, the Nazis profited tremendously by the depression.

'The results of the general election in September 1930 showed that the Nazis achieved eighteen percent of the popular vote. This result showed that Hitler's gains were made mostly at the expense of the non-Socialist parties of the middle and the right. Hitler, however, had not been unable to decrease the vote of the two Catholic parties—the Bavarian People's Party and Centre Party—or to affect the combined strength of the Socialist parties of the Left, that is the Communists and Social-Democrats.

'The most significant local election during 1931 was that of the Free State of Hesse. Unlike the other local elections, it had more than local significance. The distribution of political strength in Hesse resembled more closely the political constellation throughout the Reich. If the results of the local elections had been replicated in a general election, the Catholic parties would have obtained about fifteen per cent, the non-Socialist parties fifteen percent, the Marxist parties of the Left about thirty-five per cent, and the Nazis thirty-five per cent. The Nazis would have become the strongest party in a new Reichstag. Hitler's claims that he could get fifty percent of the popular vote enabling the Nazis to govern alone in their own right was at that stage, improbable.

'However, there was a strong possibility that if he failed to get the numbers to govern alone he could have entered into a coalition with the two Catholic parties, giving him Government.'

Zehra and Emir listened carefully. 'Just one question if I may Aidan. Could the other minority parties have entered an agreement which would stymie Hitler's ambitions?' asked Zehra.

'They could have, but they didn't. They were diametrically opposed on pretty well every issue.'

'I see. Please continue.'

'Hitler's interview with the foreign press, which he held on December 4, where he stressed his capitalistic program cooled the ardour of many of the most radical elements within the National-Socialist Party.

'However, he allayed their fears, but as a result he failed to attract influential citizens to his course. The prominent Germans who were Hitler followers could have been counted on one hand, although a few rich industrialists were included. Hitler's speeches on economic matters did win over certain business elements but alienated the radical youth who were the building blocks for the movement.

'As the latter far outnumber the former from a voting standpoint it was felt in most circles that Nazi gains in voting strength would be considerably diminished.'

'May I interrupt you again? How closely was the Nazis' manifesto aligned to the Fascists in Italy?'

'The program of Fascist Italy really had little in common with that of the Nazis in Germany. Whereas Fascism was based on the idea of a cooperative state, Nazism was based on the old Prussian idea of strong centralisation, imperialism and expansion. Their ideals were similar in that both Fascism and Nazism depend on chauvinism and was opposed to emigration. Whereas in the Nazi party the element of anti-Semitism has played a prominent role, it was entirely lacking in Fascism.

'The substance of Fascism is Mussolini's personality; the same applies to a much lesser degree to Hitler. Mussolini has the intellect and bearing of a martial hero. Hitler has the intellect of a crusading sectarian leader, oblivious to dangers which surround him but with intense energy and being relentless in the pursuit of his aims.'

'What about the trade unions? Surely without their support, he would have had very little chance of achieving his ambitions.'

'Good question Emir. It is doubtful Hitler would have succeeded in bringing the trade unions under a Nazi national dictatorship. The trade unions made up the Social-Democratic Party. They opposed a dictatorship and constituted the strongest opposition to Hitler, and the two movements were irreconcilable. The strongest of these was the trade unions controlled by the Social Democrats, which was in control of communications and the key industries. The conservative Catholic trade unions were next in strength. They constituted the Left wing of the Centre Party and were linked with the Social Democrats. The rest of the trade unions were under the control of the Communists. The workers controlled by Hitler were principally those who represented the floating labour sector, they lacked the disciplined organisational skills of the trade unionists. The trade unionists possessed a most powerful weapon the general strike. The Nazis, on the other hand, claimed that their SA troops were organised principally for the purpose of dealing with internal disorders and would be able to cope with a general strike ...'

'So it would seem Hitler had a battle in front of him to gain power?' said Zehra.

'It's wasn't a *lay down misère* for him but he had plenty of other support. Hitler, took a very strong stand to obtain the favour of international private banking groups. He promised them full payment of Germany's private debts, but not 'a cent of tribute,' that is, the cancellation of all political debts, reparations, etc. His purpose was to reassure them and, quite obviously, to gain their support in opposing the French reparations demands.'

'So where do you think Germany now stands?'

'The policies of Hitler, especially in the field of foreign affairs and the economic reform of Germany are still unclear to us.'

'Do you think war is inevitable?'

'I do.'

'Thank you, Aidan, that was a very comprehensive and informative briefing.'

Zehra and Emir left the Ambassador's office with a certain amount of trepidation. In a week's time it would be Zehra's office, Emir's office was located on the floor above.

Hitler's Fun & Games

Chapter 13

'If you don't try to win you might as well hold the Olympics in somebody's back yard.'
Jesse Owens

Franklin Tasmania 1963

'So Emir, what was it like living in Berlin in 1936? It must have been frightening in some ways, what with all the violence against the Jews and talk about war.'

'Yes, to a certain extent, although attending the Olympic Games was a real highlight.'

'You attended Hitler's games? Now that would have been an experience.'

'It was.'

1st August 1936

Olympic Games

The Embassy had organised excellent seats for Zehra and Emir.

They arrived at the Olympic stadium two hours before the official start. The detailed program they received from the Embassy looked amazing.

Parade of dignitaries to either Mass (St. Hedwig's) or a Protestant service (Evangelical Cathedral)

Olympic Flame Welcoming Ceremony at the Lustgarten with Hitler Youth

Parade of dignitaries to the Olympic Stadium

Hindenburg Airship flies over the stadium with 'XI. Olympiade Berlin 1936' painted on its side

Hitler arrives at the May Field (staging area next to the Olympic Stadium) - Olympic Fanfare by Paul Winter performed from Marathon Towers of the stadium by military band

Hitler enters the stadium to 'March of Homage' by Wagner - Hitler is greeted by small girl who salutes him with 'Heil, Mein Führer' and presents him with flowers as an Introductory Theme by Herbert Windt is performed

German National Anthem performed while every participating country's flag is raised on poles surrounding the top of the stadium

Olympic Bell rung - inscribed across it 'I summon the youth of the world'

Parade of Nations

Recording of Baron Pierre de Coubertain's voice played - the same quote used in the 1932 Olympics

Hitler declares the games open

Olympic Flag raised - simultaneously: artillery guns fire, 20,000 carrier pigeons released, fanfare played from the Marathon Towers, mass orchestra and choir perform the Olympic Hymn conducted and written by Richard Strauss

Olympic Cauldron lit by Fritz Schilgen - German 1500 meter athlete who failed to make the German team, selected for his beautiful and graceful running style

Athlete's Oath

Handel's Hallelujah Chorus performed by 3,000 singers and orchestra

Athletes parade out of the stadium followed by Concluding Fanfare by Paul Winter

Olympic Youth – mass play by Carl Diem – music by Carl Orff (performed under the floodlight at night)

Part 1: Children at Play – 2,500 girls 11-12 and 900 boys run into the stadium for the grand stairs and tunnel; dance; form the Olympic Rings; leave Part 2: Maidenly Grace – 2,300 girls 14-18 flood into the stadium; one begins a waltz; games follow with balls, hoops, and clubs; large group dance; form circle at one end of the stadium

Part 3: Youth at Play in a Serious Mood – thousands of boys flood field; sing and divide up into different national 'campfires'; fight each other; thousands of flags of all the nations enter and march around the track while boys salute; forest of flags surround the cauldron while child recites poem 'Hymn of Fire'

Part 4: Heroic Struggle and Death Lament – along the track advance dancing warriors each with a leader; leaders duel in a dance, one falls, the other wounded also falls;

leaders led off the field in death procession; mass dance 'lamentation' performed by all; Beethoven's Ninth, Fourth Mvt. begins; floodlights form a dome of light over stadium; thousands of torches and flags wave on the track during the Ode to Joy.

No other Olympic Games had such an impressive opening ceremony. This was the first Olympics to use the 'eternal flame' with runners starting at Mount Olympus and finishing in Berlin ten days later.

Zehra and Emir were close to the 'Mayfield', a grass area where the equestrian events took place; close to where Hitler and his cronies would be seated. When Hitler entered the arena the German crowd stood with their right arms outstretched yelling *'Heil Hitler'*. The intensity and excitement in the arena almost persuaded Zehra and Emir to follow suit. They could now understand how he motivated the German people and terrorised the Jews.

When the German Olympic team entered the arena the largely German crowd again rose with the Nazi salute.

When back in the quiet sanctuary of the Turkish Embassy they poured themselves a drink and reflected on what was a spectacular, yet frightening, experience.

The Turkish visitors looked forward to the first day of competition the following day. Zehra and Emir would be returning to the Olympic stadium for track and field.

Arriving at the stadium early, they took their seats ready to cheer on their Turkish heroes.

Competing were 48 competitors, 46 men and 2 women, participating in 26 events in 7 sports.

This was the most athletes Turkey had sent to an Olympic Games.

Franklin Tasmania

'Was there one moment that stood out from the rest Emir?'

'I would have to say watching Jesse Owen win his four gold medals. Another was seeing a Turkish wrestler, Yasar Erkan win gold.'

'That must have been amazing.'

'It was.'

The first gold Jesse won was in the 100 metres, where Owens edged out teammate Ralph Metcalfe in a time of 10.3 seconds.

Gold number two came the next day in the long jump, where he fouled on his first two attempts. One was just a practice run where he continued down the runway into the pit, but German officials didn't buy it and counted it as a jump. Top German long-jumper Luz Long suggested Owens play it safe and jump a few inches before the usual take-off spot. He took his advice and qualified for the finals, where he won the gold with a leap of 26 feet 5½ inches. Long was there to congratulate him.

'It took a lot of courage for him to befriend me in front of Hitler,' Owens would later say. 'You can melt down all the medals and cups I have and they wouldn't be a plating on the 24-karat friendship I felt for Luz Long at that moment.'

Luz & Jessie, Olympic Stadium

The third gold was in the 200-metre dash, where he defeated, among others, Jackie Robinson's older brother Mack, and broke the Olympic record with a time of 20.7 seconds.

Gold number four was a controversial one—not with the Germans, but with his fellow Americans. American Jews Marty Glickman and Sam Stoller were supposed to run for the United States on the 4x100 relay team. At the last minute, Owens and Metcalfe replaced them and it was reported that Hitler asked US officials not to embarrass him any further by having two Jews win gold in Berlin. Whether that's true or not, the Owens-led US team rolled to victory in a world record time of 39.8 seconds and Owens' magical Olympics came to a close.

As you're probably aware Hitler snubbed Jesse Owens. As the story goes, after Owens won one gold medal, Hitler, incensed, stormed out of Olympic Stadium so he wouldn't have to congratulate Owens on his victory.

Such a performance would have been perfectly in character, but it didn't happen. William J. Baker, Owens' biographer, says the newspapers made up the whole story. Owens himself originally insisted it wasn't true, but eventually he began saying it was, apparently out of sheer boredom with the issue.

The truth of the matter was Hitler did not congratulate Owens, but that day he didn't congratulate anybody else either, not even the German winners. As a matter of fact, Hitler didn't congratulate anyone after the first day of the competition. That first day he had shaken hands with all the German victors, but that got him in trouble with the members of the Olympic Committee. They told him that to maintain Olympic neutrality, he would have to congratulate everyone, or no one. Hitler chose to honour no one.

Zehra and Emir also attended the wrestling where Turkey won its first gold medal as well as a bronze.

The results of the 1936 Berlin Olympic Games

Country	G	S	B	Total
Germany	38	31	32	101
USA	24	21	12	57
Italy	9	13	5	27
Sweden	5	10	21	36
Finland	6	6	20	32
Japan	6	4	10	20
France	7	6	6	19
Switz	4	9	5	18
Austria	5	7	5	17
Neth	6	4	7	17
Hungary	10	1	5	16
UK	4	7	3	14
Canada	1	3	5	9
Czech	3	5	1	9
Poland	0	4	5	9
Argentina	2	2	3	7
Estonia	2	2	3	7
Norway	3	2	6	11
Denmark	0	2	3	5
Egypt	2	1	2	5
Belgium	0	0	3	3
Mexico	0	3	3	6
Latvia	0	1	1	2
Turkey	1	0	1	2

Australia	0	0	1	1
India	1	0	0	1
NZ	1	0	0	1
Phili	0	0	1	1
Portugal	0	0	1	1
Romania	0	1	0	1
SA	0	1	0	1
Yugos	1	0	1	2

Hitler got his wish: Germany dominated the medal count proving to the world Germany was a superior nation; an enormous propaganda win for the Nazis.

Patriarch of the Turks

Chapter 14

January 1938

Mustafa Ataturk was sitting in his office reading the Government correspondence for the day. He insisted on being briefed by his ministers in minute detail.

The presidential secretary knocked, entering he brought with him another red box of briefing papers.

President Mustafa Ataturk's Office

'Good morning Sir, I'm afraid I have another red box for you to read.'

'Thank you Takoda, I may not get through it all today.'

'Excuse me for asking Sir, are you feeling poorly?'

'Does it show? Yes, I'm not feeling well.'

'You seem to have become a little jaundiced, you're not your normal colour.'

'I may be coming down with the flu or something. I feel very tired, not just today but over the past week or so.'

'May I suggest I call the doctor, he may be able to give you something that will remedy the problem.'

'OK, as much as I hate doctors you can call him.'

Mustafa continued to read the Government briefs but after an hour decided he'd had enough. He left his office and headed for his bedroom for an afternoon nap.

Later that afternoon Doctor Baykara visited the presidential palace and was escorted to the President's bedroom.

Presidential Palace Ankara

Mustafa Ataturk was in his bed. The doctor approached him, noticing his jaundiced skin.

'Good afternoon Mr President, I believe you're not feeling well today?'

'No, I've felt better.'

'What seems to be the matter, Sir?'

'I just feel tired continually, no energy.'

'I see. Have you been overdoing it as it were?'

'Overdoing what exactly?'

'Work.'

'I've always got a heavy workload; I'm the President.'

'Are you eating well?'

'No, not really, I've lost my appetite lately.'

'Is there anything else unusual?'

'I can't stop itching, it's driving me crazy. I was hoping you could prescribe me a cream to ease it.'

'I'll see what I can do.'

Doctor Baykara took Mustafa's blood pressure and examined his skin, there were bruises all over his legs and arms.

'Do you normally bruise easily Mr President?'

'No, however I'm always bumping into things.'

'I'll try to get you a cream for the itching and I'll see whether I can find a tonic to lift your energy levels.'

'Well, don't take too long, I've got a lot of work to do.'

'Let me go away and think about what I can prescribe, I'll come back tomorrow morning; meanwhile, I'd like you to stay in bed.'

'Doctor, I've got a country to run. Come and see me in my office tomorrow.'

Doctor Baykara returned to his surgery at Ankara General Hospital. He decided he needed to consult with his colleague Dr Mehmed, a kidney specialist. Dr Baykara briefed his fellow clinician regarding the president's condition.

'From what you've described I would say he has cirrhosis of the liver, if it turns out to be so we need to get him to Istanbul where he can be better treated.'

Doctor Baykara made an appointment through the presidential secretary to see Mustafa the following afternoon.

The doctor was kept waiting twenty minutes before being shown into the President's office.

'Good afternoon doctor, please take a seat. I am afraid I might have wasted your time, I'm feeling much better today.'

'I'm very glad to hear that Mr President; however, the solution is not that simple.'

'What do you mean?'

'I am afraid you may have cirrhosis of the liver.'

'Is that bad?'

'It is a very serious condition, Sir.'

'So how do you treat it?'

'Sir, there isn't a treatment, nothing will cure cirrhosis or repair scarring in the liver that has already occurred.'

'There must be something you can do.'

'If we transfer you to Istanbul we may be able to delay any further liver damage. You'll have to stop drinking and smoking.'

'Forget it, I'd rather die.'

'Do you really mean that sir? What alcohol do you drink?'

'Raki of course.'

'How many do you drink a day?'

'Just the one.'

'Well that seems reasonable, one glass a day shouldn't have caused your condition.'

'One bottle doctor.'

'My God.'

'So, what do we do now?'

'As I intimated earlier you should transfer to Dolmabahce Palace in Istanbul. We can try to delay the progress of the disease more effectively.'

Dolmabahce Palace

'OK, I'll arrange it asap.'

Mustafa telephoned Zehra in Berlin requesting that she and Emir travel to Istanbul where his new presidential toy had arrived. The *Savarona* had recently been purchased and refurbished by the Turkish Government for the exclusive use of the President. It was 136 meters long and boasted 17 staterooms for Mustafa and his guests.

Savarona

Mustafa neglected to mention his physical condition to his sister, he decided to wait until she arrived in Istanbul.

Zehra and Emir arrived from Berlin early March 1938. They would be guests of Mustafa in the palace for the first few days, they would then embark on a cruise on the *Savarona* sailing and visiting the Greek islands. Before returning to Berlin they intended visiting Utopia and their other properties to ensure all was well.

After a few very pleasant days in Istanbul the presidential party boarded the magnificent yacht setting sale for the Greek Islands.

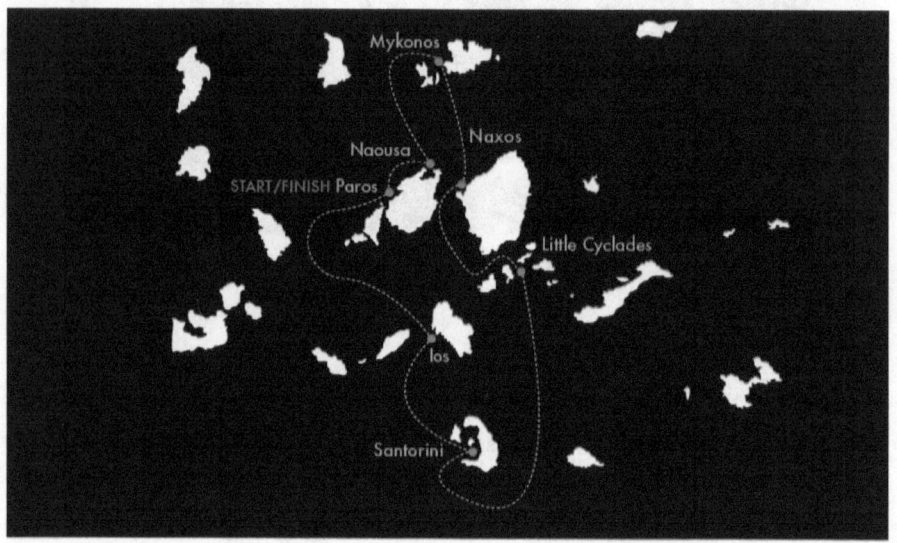

The three family members were sitting out on the sundeck enjoying a drink, the sun was shining with the temperature a warm 28 degrees.

'This is the life, you must have known we needed a break from what is happening in Berlin Mustafa.'

'Yes, I can imagine it must be tense. I have no doubt Hitler will declare war in the next twelve months. I can assure you we will be remaining neutral if he does.'

'Thank Allah for that.'

'Apart from giving you two a holiday there is something I wanted to discuss with you in person.'

'What's that brother?'

'I've been diagnosed with cirrhosis of the liver.'

'That's terrible! When were you diagnosed?'

'Last month, the doctors recommended I transfer to Istanbul for better treatment.'

'I know from my nursing days that cirrhosis is incurable.'

'Yes, so they tell me.'

'Why are you still drinking Raki?'

'Stopping now isn't going to save me so I might as well die happy.'

'Do the children know?'

'No, not yet, plenty of time.'

'Not that much time I would have thought.'

'Don't be so pessimistic Zehra.'

Mustafa Ataturk had no biological children he adopted seven daughters and one son. He was a single father.

'There's something else.'

'Yes, what is it Mustafa?'

'I am transferring you both to the embassy in Paris as soon as possible.'

'Why Paris?'

'Firstly, Berlin has become a dangerous place. Secondly I want you to save as many Turkish Jews as possible from the Nazis.'

'I'm happy to try and save the Jews,' said Emir.

'I'm sure you are considering you were born and raised a Jew.'

'How did you know that?'

'You must have known I would conduct a detailed examination of your past before giving you permission to marry Zehra.'

'You obviously have excellent intelligence.'

'Why didn't you tell me you were Jewish Emir?' asked Zehra.

'I honestly didn't think it was important.'

'Well it is now, we've got to help these poor people.'

'So I take it you're happy to transfer?'

'Absolutely, we've both seen the atrocities committed against the Jews in Berlin,' said Zehra.

Zehra and Emir returned to Berlin and arranged to transfer to Paris in April 1938.

Soon after returning to Istanbul Mustafa came down with pneumonia. By June he could scarcely stand and, after some months resting on *Savarona*, he returned to Dolmabahce Palace.

A very proud man, he refused to be seen on a stretcher. Mustafa had himself carried upstairs in an armchair, just managing to walk the last steps to his bedroom. He lapsed into a coma in September. Mustafa Kemal Ataturk died on November 10 1938.

Farewell Father

Mustafa Ataturk's death drew a gigantic outpouring of grief from the Turkish people. His body was carried through the streets of a mourning Istanbul on its way to Ankara, where it was temporarily laid to rest, while a magnificent mausoleum was erected in his memory.

Mustafa Ataturk's Funeral

Mustafa Ataturk's Mausoleum

Hitler's March to War

Chapter 15

Both Zehra and Emir sent monthly reports back to Ankara, each one more ominous than the last. It was becoming obvious that Hitler was preparing Germany for war.

Zehra received a letter from the Reich Chancellery on 15th October 1938 requesting she attend a meeting with the Chancellor Adolf Hitler. She had met other senior members of the Nazi party including Joachim von Ribbentrop several times, but to meet the Fuhrer was a whole new experience; one she wasn't eagerly awaiting.

She was instructed to go to the Reich Chancellery on 22nd October at 10 am. She presumed she would meet him in his official office.

Hitler's Meeting Area

Zehra was driven to the impressive building where the meeting would take place, her driver parked the Mercedes-Benz in the forecourt.

The young Turkish ambassador was met by a young Nazi officer who gave her the Nazi salute; she simply nodded. She was escorted up the steps into the foyer where Nazi flags adorned the walls, and a large portrait of Hitler looked down on all those that entered.

Reich Chancellery

The Turkish Ambassador was ushered into Hitler's waiting room there she waited for fifteen minutes. Finally his assistant approached Zehra, inviting her into the inner sanctum of the dictator.

Hitler rose from his desk, approaching Zehra with his hand outstretched, shaking her hand enthusiastically without being too firm. Hitler displayed obvious pleasure in meeting the Turkish ambassador.

'Hello Ambassador, please take a seat. Would you care for a coffee or tea perhaps?'

'Thank you, Chancellor, I would like a coffee please.'

'So, how are you enjoying your assignment in Berlin?'

'It's a beautiful city.'

'I believe you were here during the Olympics, did you attend?'

'Yes, my husband Emir and I attended two days at the athletics, a day at the pool and watched the Turkish wrestlers win their medals. I commend you for a wonderful event.'

'Thank you, ambassador.'

'Please call me Zehra.'

'Thank you and you can call me Chancellor.'

'Course.'

'Zehra, I believe you are the sister of the great Mustafa Kemal Ataturk?'

'Yes, that's correct.'

'I call him my shining star.'

'Why is that Chancellor?'

'He has inspired me in so many ways Zehra, I use him as a role model for the development of the Third Reich.'

'Well, next time I speak with him I'll pass on your praises.'

'Please do.'

Hitler ended the meeting, it lasted twenty minutes in all. Zehra was escorted out by his assistant and driven back to the embassy. Zehra did not mention Mustafa's medical condition to the Fuhrer.

Franklin Tasmania 1963

'Did you meet Hitler?' asked Paul.

'Yes at a couple of diplomatic functions we attended.'

'What was he like?'

'Paul, I just shook his hand then moved onto the next guest. I never had a conversation with him.'

'He must have been an imposing character.'

'Certainly, you knew when he was present.'

'So Zehra had a private meeting with Hitler?'

'She did. It was quite an experience for her.'

'I can imagine, daunting no doubt.'

'Funnily she wasn't overwhelmed, he made her feel comfortable. He was wearing a lounge suit, not his Nazi uniform, I think that eased the tension in the room.'

'When did she have her meeting with him?'

'October 22 1938.'

'My God that was just before the "*Night of Crystal.*"'

'That's right, that's when everything went pear-shaped for the Jews.'

November 1938

Kristallnacht (Night of Crystal). The sounds of breaking glass shattered the air in cities throughout Germany while fires across the country devoured synagogues and Jewish institutions. By the end of the rampage, gangs of Nazi storm troopers had destroyed seven thousand Jewish businesses, set fire to more than nine hundred synagogues, killed ninety-one Jews and deported some thirty thousand Jewish men to concentration camps.

15th March 1939

Hitler invaded and occupied Czechoslovakia in contravention of the Munich Agreement. The Nazi war machine now controlled 66 percent of Czechoslovakia's coal, 70 percent of its iron and steel, and 70 percent of its electrical power. Without those resources, the Czech nation was left vulnerable to complete German domination.

31st March 1939

Britain issued a statement guaranteeing Poland's independence. The issuing of this statement meant that if Germany invaded Poland, Britain would come to the aid of the Poles.

Berlin, September 1939

The Germans concocted a story of Polish troops crossing their border and firing on various installations. In supposed retaliation, German tanks rolled across the Polish border during the early hours of September 1st 1939. Tensions were running high throughout Europe. Britain and France began mobilisation of their armies while Italy's Mussolini desperately tried to convince Hitler to forestall war. The British and French representatives met with German Foreign Minister Ribbentrop warning that they would fulfil their obligation to Poland and go to war if German forces did not withdraw from Polish territory.

Paul Schmidt was a translator in the German Foreign Ministry and present at the history-making events of those last days of peace in Europe.

It is just after midnight on 3rd September 1939 and the German juggernaut continues to slam its way into Poland. The Germans had not responded to an earlier British and French demand to withdraw their troops and a message is received stating that Sir Neville Henderson, the British Ambassador to Germany, wishes to meet with German Foreign Minister Ribbentrop. It is obvious to all that the Ambassador's message will probably mean war. Ribbentrop decides that the translator Schmidt should meet with the British ambassador alone: he was a bit busy.

The British Embassy telephoned Schmidt to say that Henderson had received instructions from London to transmit a communication from his Government at 9 am and that he asked to be received by Ribbentrop at the Foreign Office at that time. It was clear that this communication could contain nothing agreeable, and that it might possibly be a real ultimatum. Ribbentrop in consequence showed not the slightest inclination to receive the British Ambassador personally next morning.

'Schmidt, you should receive the Ambassador in my place. Just ask the English whether that will suit them, and say that the Foreign Minister is not available at 9 o'clock.'

'The English agreed, and therefore I was instructed to receive Henderson next morning'

Schmidt described the meeting:

'On Sunday, 3rd September 1939, after the pressure of work over the last few days, I overslept, and had to take a taxi to the Foreign Office. I could just see Henderson entering the building as I drove across the Wilhelmsplatz. I used a side entrance and stood in Ribbentrop's office ready to receive Henderson punctually at 9 o'clock. Henderson was announced as the hour struck. He came in looking very serious, shook hands, but declined my invitation to be seated, remaining standing in the middle of the room. "I regret that on the instructions of my Government I have to hand you an ultimatum for the German Government," he said with deep emotion and then, with both of us still standing, he read out the British ultimatum.'

'More than twenty-four hours have elapsed since an immediate reply was requested to the warning of 1st September and since then the attacks on Poland have been intensified. If His Majesty's Government has not received satisfactory assurances of the cessation of all aggressive action against Poland, and the withdrawal of German troops from that country by 11 o'clock British Summer Time, from that time a state of war will exist between Great Britain and Germany.'

'When he had finished reading, Henderson handed me the ultimatum and bade me goodbye, saying: "I am sincerely sorry that I must hand such a document to you in particular, as you have always been most anxious to help."

'I too expressed my regret, and added a few heartfelt words. I always had the highest regard for the British Ambassador.

Ambassador Henderson Leaving the German Foreign Office

'I then took the ultimatum to the Chancellery, where everyone was anxiously awaiting me. Most of the members of the Cabinet and the leading men of the Party were collected in the room next to Hitler's office. There was something of a crush and I had difficulty in getting through to Hitler.

Hitler Seated at His Desk

'When I entered the next room Hitler was sitting at his desk and Ribbentrop stood by the window. Both looked up expectantly as I came in. I stopped at some distance from Hitler's desk, and then slowly translated the British

Government's ultimatum. When I finished, there was complete silence.

'Hitler sat immobile, gazing before him. He was not at a loss, as was afterwards stated, nor did he rage as others allege. He sat completely silent and unmoving.

'After an interval, which seemed an age, he turned to Ribbentrop, who had remained standing by the window. "What now?" asked Hitler with a savage look, as though implying that his Foreign Minister had misled him about England's probable reaction? Ribbentrop answered quietly: "I assume that the French will hand in a similar ultimatum within the hour."

'As my duty was now performed, I withdrew. To those in the anteroom pressing round me I said: 'The English have just handed us an ultimatum. In two hours a state of war will exist between England and Germany.'

'In the anteroom, too, this news was followed by complete silence. Goering turned to me and said: 'If we lose this war, then God have mercy on us!' Goebbels stood in a corner, downcast and self-absorbed. Everywhere in the room I saw looks of grave concern, even amongst the lesser Party people.'

I Love Paris
but
Not in War Time

Chapter 16

June 1, 1939

Zehra and Emir arrived in Paris aboard the Orient Express, a journey of two days.

The trip gave the two diplomats time to relax and prepare themselves for their new assignment. The fact that Turkey had made it clear to all that it would remain neutral if war was declared made the prospect of the Germans invading France more tolerable.

An embassy car met them at Gare du Nord railway station, transporting the couple to the Turkish embassy at 44 Rue de Sevres where a four bedroom apartment had been allocated to them.

Turkish Embassy Paris

Zehra and Emir settled into their new abode. They had a week before officially taking up their diplomatic duties. They used this time to see the sights of Paris. Neither of them had visited the city of lights before, they fell in love with the magnificent metropolis.

Zehra began her ambassadorial role while Emir was assigned immigration in addition to his position as military attaché.

Many Turkish citizens were becoming fearful of a Nazi invasion, they were aware of what had been happening in Germany since the "Night of Crystal".

Emir was interviewing more than ten people a day issuing them with the appropriate papers enabling the Turkish Jews to return to their homeland.

September 1939

Zehra, along with the rest of the world, was alarmed when Hitler and Stalin signed a non-aggression pact.

On August 23, 1939 Nazi Germany and the Soviet Union signed a German-Soviet Non-aggression Pact, in which the two countries agreed to take no military action against each other for the following 10 years. With Europe on the brink of another major war, Soviet leader Joseph Stalin viewed the pact as a way to keep his nation on peaceful terms with Germany, while giving him time to build up the Soviet military. German chancellor Adolf Hitler used the pact to make sure Germany was able to invade Poland unopposed. The pact also contained a secret agreement in which the Soviets and Germans agreed how they would later divide up Eastern Europe. The German-Soviet Non-aggression Pact collapsed in June 1941, when German forces invaded the Soviet Union

September 1 1939

September was a cataclysmic month in Europe:

September 1, 1939–Nazis invade Poland (Jewish pop. 3.35 million, the largest in Europe). Beginning of SS activity in Poland.

September 1, 1939–Jews in Germany are forbidden to be outdoors after 8 p.m. in winter and 9 p.m. in summer.

September 3, 1939–Great Britain and France declare war on Germany.

September 4, 1939–the German Army cuts off Warsaw.

September 17, 1939–Soviet troops invade eastern Poland.

September 21, 1939–Heydrich issues instructions to S.S. in Poland regarding treatment of Jews, stating they are to be gathered into ghettos near railroads for the future "final goal." He also orders a census and the establishment of Jewish administrative councils within the ghettos to implement Nazi policies and decrees.

September 23, 1939–German Jews are forbidden to own radios.

September 27, 1939–Warsaw surrenders.

September 29, 1939–Nazis and Soviets divide up Poland. Over two million Jews reside in Nazi controlled areas, leaving 1.3 million in the Soviet area.

In September–Quote from Nazi newspaper, Der Stürmer, published by Julius Streicher – 'The Jewish people ought to be exterminated root and branch. Then the plague of pests would have disappeared in Poland at one stroke.'

Paris Falls May, 1940

After German troops invaded Poland in September 1939, Britain and France declared war on Nazi Germany. Despite this, there were no major battles between the three countries for several months, the so-called "Sitzkrieg" or "phony war." That changed drastically with the German invasion of France in May 1940. In six short weeks, the Germans defeated the French Army, taking almost two million prisoners. On June 14th, the Nazis occupied Paris. French Prime Minister Paul Reynaud resigned on June 16th, and was replaced by World War I hero Marshal Phillipe Petain, who asked the Germans for an armistice. The agreement was signed on June 22nd. According to the terms of the agreement, the North of France would be occupied by the Germans; the rest of the country would remain nominally independent, but a de facto German puppet state, with its capital in Vichy.

EXODUS

Chapter 17

Paris 1942

Philippe Kahn was regarded as one of the pre-eminent jewellers in Paris. His shop was located in the prestigious Arcades des Champs Elysées. Léonard Rosenthal a French businessman, diamond merchant, and property developer, had built the arcade in 1925.

Philippe's fine jewellery was sought by Parisian high society for many years however the occupation of Paris by Nazi Germany had limited his clientele's purchasing ability. He still manufactured rings and bracelets however they were of much more simple design.

His life had changed as it had for all Parisians, however, he had to contend with one more complication—Philippe was Jewish, as were his wife and four children. There were an estimated 150,000 Jewish nationals living in France prior to the invasion, this figure rose to 330,000 due to the United States and the United Kingdom refusing to accept any more Jewish refugees. Many of these Jews had fled from Poland and Eastern Europe to what they thought a safe refuge.

Philippe and his wife were Turkish by birth, they immigrated to France in 1920 soon after the First World War.

Turkey had declared itself neutral and therefore insisted all the Turkish Jews in German-occupied Europe be allowed to return safely to their home country. Over 20,000 Turkish Jews resided in France.

The German SS had entered the store several times harassing the jeweller and his customers but leaving without arresting him. They were under orders not to deport Turkish nationals for the time being.

Friday, June 6, 1942

Philippe and Ruth and their four children had returned from the Synagogue and were preparing for their Sabbath dinner.

The table was set in the traditional manner, after prayers they began their meal

'The SS visited the shop again yesterday warning me not to have any loose diamonds in stock,' said Philippe.

'Why not? How do they expect you to carry on doing business without diamonds? That would be like telling a butcher he couldn't stock meat.'

'I suspect they think we could sell stones to other Jews which could be traded for transport out of France.'

'This is getting ridiculous Philippe, I think we should consider returning to Turkey.'

'We would have to walk away from our home and our business, we wouldn't have two Francs to rub together.'

'We'd have our lives our children and our dignity, surely that's worth the sacrifice.'

'OK, I'll go to the Turkish embassy on Monday.'

'I think that would be for the best,' responded Ruth.

The cab pulled up outside the imposing embassy building. Philippe paid the taxi driver and climbed the marble steps entering the vast entrance foyer. He caught sight of a sign indicating that immigration was located on the first floor. When Philippe reached the immigration office he was taken aback, there must have been 100 people in the line. He had arrived at the embassy at 9 am he got to see the immigration officer at 4 pm.

At last, his name was called. He approached the desk where a distinguished looking man was seated.

'Hello, my name is Emir Saatchi, how may I help you?'

'Hello, I am Philippe Kahn. I would like to return my family to Turkey.'

'I see Philippe, when did you arrive in France?'

'My wife Ruth and I arrived in 1920.'

'Have you maintained your Turkish citizenship while here?'

'I have to confess I haven't, we both thought we would never return to Turkey.'

'That makes things a little harder.'

'Does it mean we can't return?'

'Not necessarily Philippe, but it means I have to work a little harder to get your return approved by the German authorities. Is Philippe you're real name?'

'No, I changed it when we first arrived in Paris, I thought Philippe was less conspicuous.'

'So, what is your Turkish name?'

'Saladin.'

'Good, we'll use your real name when we draw up the papers. It will now be as you say less conspicuous to the Nazi authorities.'

'So, what needs to happen now?'

'I have to arrange the appropriate forms for you and your family.'

'You can do this?'

'Yes, I can. I have all your details, leave it with me, I will contact you when things have been finalised.'

'Thank you so much.'

'My pleasure.'

Emir arranged to have the appropriate papers drawn up including the Turkish passports for the Kahn family as well as thirty other families who would be joining them on the "train caravan".

Train Caravan was the term used for the trains that departed Paris transporting Jews back to Turkey. The journey was often hindered by the Croats, Serbians and Bulgarians as the locomotives passed through these countries on the way to Turkey. None of these Eastern European nations was sympathetic to the plight of the Jews fleeing the Nazi death camps. Despite bureaucratic obstructions, the trains were eventually given freedom of passage.

The Embassy notified Saladin that he and his family were booked to depart Gare du Nord station on Saturday September, 1. He was instructed to pick up the family's travel documents and emigration papers at the embassy on August 28, at 2 pm.

Saladin was both delighted on the one hand and disappointed on the other. The thought of leaving Paris after all these years saddened him however he knew he and his family must leave.

The jeweller collected the loose diamonds he had hidden away over the past twelve months and took them home. Ruth sewed the stones into the family's clothing, she was able to hide 100 small diamonds. It wasn't a sultan's fortune, but it would be enough to establish the business in Istanbul once they arrived.

August 28

Philippe aka Saladin arrived at the embassy fifteen minutes early, the number of Turks waiting in the anteroom hadn't diminished. He waited until 2.20 pm, finally he heard his name, Mr Saladin Kahn.

'Good afternoon Mr Saatchi.'

'Good afternoon Mr Kahn.'

'Please, call me Philippe.'

'I'd rather call you Saladin. You can call me Emir.'

'Sorry, I'm still coming to grips with the change of name.'

'Now that we have that out of the way let's get down to business. I have six passports and the departure documents you will need to show not only the German authorities but the border posts along your route. I wish you and your family well Saladin, maybe sometime in the future we can meet again in Istanbul.'

'Thank you for all that you've done for me and my family Emir we appreciate it.'

Saladin caught a taxi home; calling the family together he explained to the children Pierre 16, Anna 14, Sophie 12 and Henry 10 the reason why they were about to leave France bound for Turkey. Despite their ages, they were more than aware of what was happening within the Jewish community in Paris. Several of their friends had been deported to Poland.

September 1, 1942

The Kahn family caught two taxis to the railway station they couldn't fit the entire luggage in just one. At Gare du Nord they secured a porter and made their way to platform ten, they passed many German SS soldiers on the way. Saladin was ordered to present their documents on three occasions. Finally, they made it to the platform where a locomotive with 15 carriages was waiting for them.

Saladin found their carriage it was spacious, but it wasn't a sleeper, they would be sitting up for the three-day journey.

Once settled the children waited for the trip to begin. At 3 pm they all heard the whistle, the adventure was about to commence.

Apart from some delays at the borders the trip was uneventful, the children amused themselves reading books and playing cards. Saladin and Ruth used the time to discuss their future and how best to re-establish their lives in Istanbul.

September 4, 1942

The train pulled into the Sirkeci Railway Station in Istanbul at 10 am. The children were excited, Saladin and Ruth were apprehensive.

The couple did have relatives in the city but had no idea how to contact them, they were alone and without accommodation. The family was standing at the entrance to the railway station not sure where they were going to stay when a man approached them.

'Good morning Mr and Mrs Khan, my name is Izzet Bucak, Mr Saatchi sent me to meet you and take you to your accommodation.'

'Emir organised a place for us to stay?'

'He did, please follow me my car is around the corner. Let me help you with your luggage.'

Izzet led them to his car a black Mercedes Benz large enough to fit the family and their luggage. Once settled in the limousine, he drove through the streets of Istanbul past Sophia and the Blue Mosque arriving at their destination twenty minutes later. Saladin was confused, the building where they parked was not a hotel it looked more like an apartment block.

'Ok we are here. I'll show you the apartment then we can get your luggage.'

The Khan family followed Izzet up to the first floor, he unlocked the apartment indicating they should enter.

They were astounded, it was a beautifully decorated apartment with four bedrooms and spacious living areas. There was a large deck overlooking a manicured garden at the rear.

'This is magnificent Izzet, did Emir indicate how long we can stay here?'

'No, he didn't mention it to me, sir. You will have to ask him yourself.'

Emir and Zehra maintained the apartment for when they visited Istanbul while they lived at Tekirdag. It was now used for families such as Saladin's to aid them to get re-established in Istanbul. The Khan's would stay there for three months. The jeweller leased a small shop in the Grand Bazaar trading as "The House of Khan".

Road to Nowhere

Auschwitz

Chapter 18

August 5, 1943

Emir was finalising the immigration papers for a group of 100 Turkish nationals who were due to board the Caravan Train departing for Istanbul on August 8.

Zehra rushed into Emir's office.

'Emir I've just discovered that the Jews due to depart Paris on the 8th have been rounded up by the Germans and are being deported to Poland.'

'Poland?'

'Auschwitz.'

'They can't do that, we have an agreement with the German administration.'

'Well, they think they can, in fact, they've done it.'

'We'll see about that. You stay here darling, I'll go and sort it out, it's probably just a mistake.'

Emir called for the embassy driver to transport him to Gare du Nord Railway Station. He had discovered the train was due to depart at 4 pm. He arrived at the station thirty minutes before departure time. There were open carriages as far as the eye could see all loaded with people destined to die at the end of their journey.

He searched for the German officer in charge, he found him smoking in the departure lounge.

'Hello Colonel Hartmann, my name is Emir Saatchi, I am the Turkish Military Attaché and Senior Immigration Officer.'

'Yes, how can I help you?'

'I believe you have approximately 100 Turkish nationals aboard this train. Under our agreement with the German Government, Turkish Jews are exempt from deportation.'

Jews Bound for Auschwitz

'Is that right? Well, it's taken three hours to load this filthy scum onto the wagons I don't intend to take any Jews off. I don't even know which wagons they could be on.'

'If you give me thirty minutes sir I'm sure I can locate them.'

'Why are you so desperate to save these people for God sake? They're fucking Jews.'

'I am a Jew.'

'Are you? Well in that case you can join them.'

The German officer ordered two men to take Emir and squeeze him into a carriage. Five minutes later the train to Auschwitz departed Paris.

Emir had no room to move, 200 people were squeezed into a wagon that could take 50 comfortably. There was no fresh water, a bucket at one end of the wagon served as a toilet. He tried to come to terms with the fact he was a senior Turkish diplomat on his way to a Nazi death camp.

Zehra was informed by the embassy driver what had happened at the train station; she was horrified.

She telephoned Carl-Heinrich von Stülpnagel, Military Commander of Paris to demand Emir's return and that of the Turkish nationals on board the death train.

General von Stülpnagel was aware that Zehra was the sister of the late Mustafa Kemal Ataturk, he also knew how much the Fuhrer had admired the Turkish leader. He decided to act, issuing orders to stop the train and release the Turkish Military Attaché and the Turkish Jews. He didn't want to anger Hitler.

The train was held at Reims Station until the transport trucks arrived to take Emir and the Turkish Jews back to Paris. Once offloaded the train continued its journey to Auschwitz.

Auschwitz

The army trucks sent to collect the Turkish Jews arrived back in Paris at midnight Emir had informed them that their papers were all in order. He advised the Turks to stay in the embassy sleeping in makeshift accommodation until they could, under Turkish guard, make their way to the railway station. The Caravan Train was scheduled to depart at 11 am.

Trucks Departing Reims

Franklin Tasmania 1963

'That must have been terrifying Emir, you were on your way to certain death.'

'It was, the most horrible part of it all was looking at the faces of all the people in the wagon with me. The look of sheer desperation and hopelessness on their faces.'

'Were you aware what awaited you at Auschwitz?'

'We knew that death camps existed, and Auschwitz was by far the largest, so yes the embassy was aware of Hitler's Final Solution. That's why we worked so hard to repatriate the Turkish Jews.'

'It just beggars belief what the Germans did to the Jews during the war.'

'It wasn't just the Jews, they also exterminated Gypsies, Communists, and the disabled. They also exterminated 3,000,000 Russian POWs and about 2,000,000 Poles. What many people don't know is they were also murdered homosexuals, Freemasons and Jehovah's Witnesses. They slaughtered anybody they felt posed a threat to the Reich.'

'Thank God your wife acted as she did.'

'Absolutely, I wouldn't be here having dinner with you now if she hadn't.'

'How many Jews did you repatriate back to Turkey Emir?'

'Close to 20,000.'

'That's fantastic, you effectively saved the lives of 20,000 people.'

'It had to be done. Zehra and I were passionate about it, that's why we took on the roles we did in Paris.'

'When did you both go back to Turkey?'

'When Charles de Gaulle and the Americans marched into Paris, not literally but not long before Germans surrendered.'

'I take it your business continued to grow, throughout the war years?'

'No, it didn't grow, but it didn't contract either.'

'You were able to return and take up the mantle as it were.'

'Yes, Zehra and I decided it was time to leave the diplomatic service and concentrate on building Arilik.'

'You only had the one boy Emir?'

'Yes, Zehra and I were both keen to start a family but alas, it wasn't meant to be. When we realised we couldn't have children of our own we decided to adopt.'

'So you adopted, just like Mustafa?'

'Yes, although Mustafa adopted seven, we only adopted one.'

'You mentioned he died.'

'I'd rather not talk about it, it still breaks my heart.'

'Sorry, I understand.'

'Do you have children?'

'Yes, two sons.'

'How old are they?'

'Ian is 16, and Craig is 13.'

'You must be very proud Paul.'

'I am Emir, both boys are doing well academically as well as at sport; they're good kids.'

'You're lucky living in Australia, there must be plenty of opportunities.'

'Yes, I agree it's a great country to bring up a family.'

'Well Paul, I think the waitress wants to go home, I believe we should leave. I have to get up early also as I have a plane to catch.'

'You're flying out tomorrow?'

'Yes, I'm afraid I have to get back to Turkey, I have a business to run. You should consider bringing your family to Turkey for a holiday sometime.'

'We might just do that Emir. It was great to meet you and hear your fascinating story.'

'It was a pleasure to meet you Paul; goodbye.'

'Goodbye Emir.'

Planning Hitler's Demise

Chapter 19

Zehra and Emir spent a significant amount of time organising 'train caravans' to transport Jews back to Turkey. This action was encouraged by the Vichy government as well as the French authorities in German-occupied France as the only way to make sure that Turkish Jews were not subjected to the anti-Jewish laws. The Nazi occupation officials themselves were increasingly unhappy about the exemptions and were regularly demanding that they end. Thus the French Foreign Ministry wrote to the Turkish Embassy at Vichy on 13 January 1943, after the French finally had accepted the Turkish argument that it was illegal for them to discriminate among Turkish citizens of different religions:

'To avoid the application of these measures to Turkish citizens, the Ministry of Foreign Affairs would be disposed to look favourably on the return of the interested parties to their countries of origin.'

In the middle of 1943, the Nazi occupying authorities, inspired by Adolph Eichmann, finally issued an ultimatum to Turkey and other neutral countries that they would have to repatriate all their Jewish citizens in France, after which all those who remained would be treated the same as French Jews.

Most of the neutral countries agreed to this immediately evacuating their Jews quickly as they could be sent them home directly without passing through third countries. Turkey was unable to do the same because with the Mediterranean closed to shipping, the only way to send Turkish Jews back was by train through South-eastern Europe. The Nazis issued group visas for the Jews. However, the various countries located along the path of the trains were not at all anxious to help Jews escape extermination. The most notorious of these were Croatia, Serbia and Bulgaria, which caused many difficulties to prevent the trains from passing through their territory on their way to Turkey. Finally, however, the Turkish diplomats were able to organise four train caravans during 1943 and eight more in 1944, which together transported some 2,000 Jews to Istanbul.

Other significant things were happening in Europe in 1943 the Allies were planning their invasion of Europe.

Stalin, Roosevelt and Churchill

President Roosevelt was feeling shattered after the seven-thousand-mile journey to Tehran to meet with Winston Churchill and Joseph Stalin.

He suffered from polio, which confined him to a wheelchair for most of the time, but it was not this condition that taxed his energy levels; it was cardiovascular disease consisting of congestive heart failure, hypertension, and hypertensive heart disease. It was his heart that would lead to his death less than eighteen months later.

The conference was scheduled to convene at 16:00 on 28th November 1943. Stalin arrived early, followed by Roosevelt, who was wheeled in.

Churchill, taking his time strolling and smoking his signature cigar, came half an hour later.

The two principal Western powers had agreed that their primary objective was to ensure full cooperation and assistance from the Soviet Union for their war policies. Stalin agreed, but with conditions: Stalin pressed for a revision of Poland's eastern border with the Soviet Union to match the line set by British Foreign Secretary Lord Curzon in 1920. To compensate Poland for the resulting loss of territory, the three leaders agreed to move the German-Polish border to the Oder and Neisse rivers.

Roosevelt, Churchill, and Stalin then moved on to other more pressing matters, namely the cross-Channel invasion of occupied France by the Western Allies (Operation Overlord) and general war policy. Operation Overlord was scheduled to begin in May 1944, in conjunction with a Soviet attack on Germany's eastern border.

Roosevelt gave Stalin a pledge that he had been waiting for since June 1941: that the British and the Americans would open a second front in France in the spring of 1944. Churchill up to this point had been seeking a joint United Kingdom, United States and Commonwealth forces initiative through the Mediterranean that would have secured British interests in the Middle East and India. The three leaders agreed that the nations in league with the Axis powers would be divided into territories to be controlled by the Soviet Union, the US, and the UK.

Iran and Turkey were discussed in detail; they all agreed to support Iran's government, as addressed in the following declaration:

The Three Governments realise that the war has caused special economic difficulties for Iran. They all agreed that they would continue to make available to the Government of Iran such economic assistance as may be possible, having regard to the heavy demands made upon them by their world-wide military operations.

The declaration issued by the three leaders on conclusion of the conference on 1st December 1943, recorded the following military conclusions:

• The Yugoslav Partisans should be supported by supplies and equipment and also by commando operations.

• It would be desirable if Turkey should come into the war on the side of the Allies before the end of the year. Noted Stalin's statement that if Turkey found herself at war with Germany, and as a result, Bulgaria declared war on Turkey or attacked her, the Soviet Union would immediately be at war with Bulgaria.

•The Conference further took note that this could be mentioned in the forthcoming negotiations to bring Turkey into the war.

•The cross-Channel invasion of France (Operation Overlord) would be launched during May 1944, in conjunction with an operation against southern France. The latter operation would be undertaken in as great strength as the availability of landing craft permitted.

• The Conference also took note of Marshal Stalin's statement that the Soviet forces would launch an offensive at about the same time with the object of preventing the German forces from transferring from the Eastern to the Western Front.

• Agreed that the military staffs of the Three Powers should keep in close touch with each other regarding the impending operations in Europe. In particular, it was decided that a cover plan to mystify and mislead the enemy as regards these actions should be concerted between the staffs concerned.

The team at Bletchley Park were given the task of fooling Hitler and his army about the exact location of the invasion through false and misleading Enigma messages. This exercise would form a significant part of 'Operation Fortitude'.

'Operation Fortitude' was the code name for the military deception employed by the Allied nations in the context of an overall deception strategy (code named Bodyguard) during the build-up to the D-Day landings. 'Fortitude' was divided into two sub-plans, North and South, with the aim of misleading the German high command as to the location of the imminent invasion.

Both North and South plans involved the creation of fake field armies based in Edinburgh and the south of England. The first army threatened Norway–Fortitude North; and the second Pas de Calais–Fortitude South.

Operation Fortitude was intended to divert Hitler's attention away from Normandy and, after the successful invasion on 6th June 1944, delay reinforcement by convincing the Germans that the landings were purely a diversionary attack.

Operation Fortitude

It was initially envisioned that deception would occur through five main channels:

Physical deception: to mislead the enemy with non-existent units through fake infrastructure and equipment, such as dummy landing craft, dummy airfields, tanks and decoy lighting.

Controlled leaks of information through diplomatic channels to the Germans.

Wireless traffic: to mislead the enemy, wireless traffic was created to simulate actual units.

Use of German agents controlled by the Allies through the Double Cross System to send false information to the German intelligence services.

The public presence of notable staff associated with phantom groups, such as FUSAG (First US Army Group), most notably the well-known US General George S. Patton.

Placing False Tank into Position

Operation Bodyguard and its sub-operations, including Fortitude, fooled the Nazis into spreading their defensive forces over several locations thus weakening their military strength.

The Bletchley Park team had managed to confuse the Germans and its allies with the cracked codes from the Enigma machine. Alan Turing and his magnificent bombe (computer) had enabled the Allies to invade mainland Europe and begin the annihilation of Hitler and the Nazis.

I Do Like a Day Beside the Seaside

But Not Omaha or Juno

Chapter 21

Emir was aware he had relatives who had emigrated from Hungary to the United States in the late eighteenth century just as his family had immigrated to Australia. However, he wasn't aware that his second cousin Peter Jacobson from Brooklyn New York was a Captain in the American army. Nor was he mindful of the fact that Captain Jacobson was about to play a significant role in the liberation of France.

Captain Peter Jacobson had recently qualified from Harvard Medical School and immediately enlisted in the US Marines following a long line of Jacobsons before him. After training he was assigned to the Marine Headquarters in England.

On 4th June 1944, he was ordered to report to the commander of the First Infantry Division, Major General Clarence R. Huebner.

'Captain, we are about to embark on a mission that will turn the course of the war. We are about to take back France and after that, all the territory between the French coast and Berlin. It's not going to be easy and we will suffer many casualties. It will be your job and the job of all the medical teams to ensure the wounded are either treated where they fall, or transported to the hospital ships for more serious medical attention. I wish you well. Keep your bloody head down.'

'Thank you, sir. I shall try and stay in one piece. When are we due to leave?'

'Tomorrow.'

The weather was not conducive for such a massive operation and the fleet was forced to return. The next day, 6th June, the armada set sail for France heading for the Normandy coast.

D Day

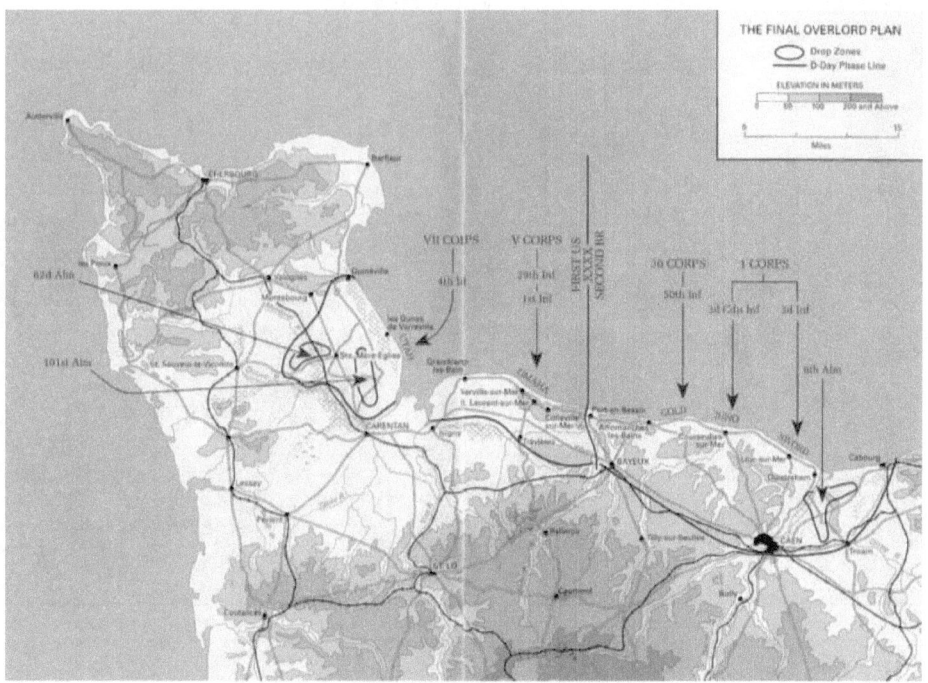

'They came, rank after relentless rank, ten lanes wide, twenty miles across, five thousand ships of every description. There were fast new attack transports, slow rust-scarred freighters, small ocean liners, Channel steamers, hospital ships, weather-beaten tankers, coasters and swarms of fussing tugs. There were endless columns of shallow-draft landing ships—great wallowing vessels, some of them almost 350 feet long. ... Ahead of the convoys were processions of minesweepers, Coast Guard cutters, buoy-layers and motor launches. Barrage balloons flew above the ships. Squadrons of fighter planes weaved below the clouds. And surrounding this fantastic cavalcade of ships packed with men, guns, tanks, motor vehicles and supplies, ... was a formidable array of 702 warships.'

"The Longest Day"–*Cornelius Ryan*

One hundred and sixty thousand Allied troops landed along a fifty-mile stretch of heavily fortified French coastline to confront Nazi Germany on the beaches of Normandy, France.

General Dwight D. Eisenhower called the operation a crusade in which *'we will accept nothing less than full victory.'* More than five thousand ships and thirteen thousand aircraft supported the D-Day invasion. By day's end the Allies gained a foothold in Normandy. The D-Day toll was extremely high; more than nine thousand Allied soldiers were killed or wounded.

One hundred thousand soldiers began the march across Europe to defeat Hitler.

Omaha Beach

Omaha Beach interconnected the US and British beaches. It was a critical link between the Cotentin Peninsula and the flat plain in front of Caen. Omaha was also the most restricted and heavily defended beach: for this reason, the experienced US First Division was assigned to land there. The terrain was very steep. Omaha Beach was unlike any of the other assault beaches in Normandy. Its crescent curve and unusual assortment of bluffs, cliffs and draws were immediately recognisable from the sea. It was the most defensible beach chosen for the D-Day landing. There was the strong opinion that it would be too difficult to land there, and too many casualties would result. The high ground commanded all approaches to the beach from the sea and tidal flats, making the Allied troops easy targets for the German machine guns. To make matters worse were the narrow passages between the bluffs. Advances directly up the steep bluffs were difficult in the extreme. German machine-gun nests were arranged to command all the approaches and the concrete pillboxes were sited to fire east and west; thereby exposing the Allied troops while the Germans remained concealed from bombarding warships. These pillboxes had to be taken out by direct assault. Compounding this problem was the failure of Allied intelligence to identify a nearly full-strength infantry division, the 352nd, directly behind the beach. Intelligence had them located more than twenty kilometres inland.

Captain Peter Jacobson was at the back of the LCA (Landing Craft Assault) when it hit the beach, the ramp dropped, and the Marines waded through the water and up onto the beach.

Bullets and shells were raining down on the invading troops. Soldiers and Marines were falling, the sand stained with the blood of the wounded and dead.

Peter started up the beach. He saw a wounded Marine crawling towards the cliff face. He crouched down beside him and asked to look at the wound. The young Marine pointed to his stomach. Peter lifted his shirt and saw a small hole in the centre of his abdomen. He rolled the young man over to see his back. It was as Peter suspected the exit wound was as big as his fist. This marine wasn't going home. Peter could do no more than reassure him and make him as comfortable as possible in the circumstances.

Peter kept crawling up the beach, dodging bullets and shells. He couldn't believe the number of dead littering the landing area. The medic spotted another

Marine; this time wounded in the leg. He was able to apply a bandage and called for the stretcher-bearers to take him to the LCA for transfer to the hospital ship. His knee had been shattered.

Peter was not overly religious, but seeing the mayhem around him, the dead, the dying, the wounded crying out in pain, he thought 'If there is a hell his is what it must be like.'

The young Captain and his team managed to transfer twenty wounded to the hospital ship. The LCA was now on its way back for the next batch.

Photo # 80-G-252558   Scene on Omaha Beach soon after the landings there, June 1944

The young captain had been on duty for twenty-three hours, collecting the wounded and transferring them to the hospital ship for extensive treatment. He and his medical team also tended the wounded on the beach, stitching and bandaging the frightened young soldiers and sending them on their way to who knows what.

Two LCAs laden with American wounded received direct hits from the German artillery. Their second chance was obliterated in seconds.

Omaha Beach 7th June

Captain Jacobson returned to Omaha Beach the next day; there were spent shells and bullets littering the sand.

Bodies of Allied soldiers remained where they had fallen, distorted and bloodied, a grim reminder of what had transpired the day before.

Peter's orders were to follow his company inland and establish a dressing station to tend the wounded. The team were able to scale the cliffs using rope ladders and made their way inland. They found an old farmhouse, which Peter decided, would be suitable for the station.

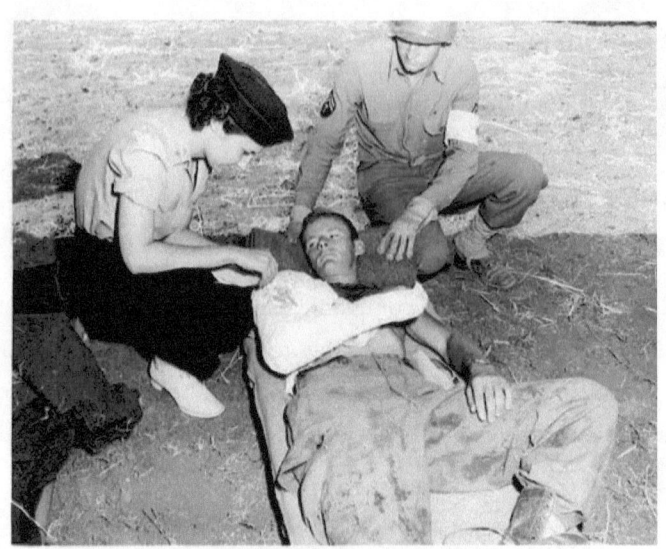

Medics Attending a Wounded Marine at Omaha

Once the dressing station had been established the medical team waited for the wounded to arrive. They didn't have to wait long–a constant stream of soldiers began to materialise, most of them being carried by stretcher-bearers, others were the walking wounded.

The VII Corps advanced westwards to cut off the Cotentin Peninsula. An additional three infantry divisions had landed to reinforce the Corps. Major General J. Lawton Collins, the Corps Commander, drove his troops hard, replacing units in the front lines or sacking officers if progress was slow.

The medical teams, including Peter's, were having trouble keeping up the pace. No sooner had they established a new dressing station than they would have to pack up and move forward. The wounded were taken back to Omaha Beach to be transported to the already overcrowded hospital ships.

By day six C-46 and C-47 cargo planes were flying across the English Channel to land on improvised runways on the Normandy beachhead.

The planes ferried badly wounded men to hospitals in Great Britain. It was the job of the flight nurses to take care of the twenty-four wounded soldiers each plane could carry. Some men were missing arms or legs; others had head or chest wounds.

The Germans facing VII Corps were a mix of regiments and battle groups from several divisions, many of which had already suffered heavy casualties fighting the American airborne troops in the first days of the landings. Very few German armoured or mobile troops could be sent to this part of the front because of the threat to Caen further east. Infantry reinforcements arrived, but slowly.

By 16th June there were no further natural obstacles in front of the American forces. The German command was in some confusion. General Rommel and other commanders wished to withdraw their troops in good order into the Atlantic Wall fortifications of Cherbourg, where they could have withstood a siege for some time. Adolf Hitler, issuing orders from his headquarters in East Prussia, demanded that they hold their present lines even though this risked disaster.

Captain Jacobson was transferred to the 79th Division as they had lost a significant percentage of their medical Corps in the fighting. Two days later, Peter's new battalion and a significant contingent of men and machinery from other Divisions, were on the outskirts of Cherbourg.

Major General Lawton Collins was in charge of the operation. He was confident they would be able to take Cherbourg in the next twenty-four hours. However, Lieutenant General Karl-Wilhelm von Schlieben, the German garrison commander defending the port city, thought otherwise. He had twenty-one thousand men at his disposal, however; they were either inexperienced or totally exhausted. Food, fuel and ammunition were short.

'I know that Hitler will send us reinforcements any day now. We just have to hold out until then,' Von Schlieben assured his second-in-command.

'What are our exact orders, General Von Schlieben?'

'The Führer has demanded that we fight to the death.'

Later that day, as the US troops were progressing towards the city, German planes were seen overhead. But they were not dropping much needed supplies-Hitler had ordered they drop Iron Crosses to be awarded to the brave men of Cherbourg.

'Fight to the last man. I think we'll have to,' Von Schlieben complained.

Major General Collins issued a demand to the Germans to surrender the city and save many German and Allied lives but General Von Schlieben refused, based on orders from Hitler.

Collins subsequently launched a general assault on 22nd June. Resistance was stiff at first, but the Americans slowly cleared the Germans from their bunkers and concrete pillboxes. On 26th June, the 79th Division captured Fort du Roule, which dominated the city and its defences. This finished any organised defence. Von Schlieben was captured. The harbour fortifications and the arsenal surrendered a few days later, after a token resistance. Some German troops, cut off outside the defences, held out until 1st July.

Captain Jacobson and his team marched into Cherbourg, along with twenty-five thousand US troops.

Hitler was devastated and held Von Schlieben responsible as a very poor role model and leader.

By July the 79th Division had taken Lessay, crossed the Sarthe River and in early August entered Le Mans. In September they had moved east to the Franco-Belgian border frontier and crossed the Moselle River. Casualties were high and the logistics for evacuating the wounded weren't getting any easier.

The Division was given time off after such an arduous and costly few months. The Division regrouped, refreshed and readied itself to march into Germany. They moved across the Moder River in November, and through Haguenau. In December they encountered the Siegfried Line. From December until early February 1945, the Division fought many engagements around the Moder, most of them defensive until they were able to go on the offensive again.

Peter and his team were attending the wounded in the dressing station when a hail of bullets went through the station. Several of the wounded were hit as well as one of the nurses. Peter received a wound to the right leg just above the knee and another to his hip. His medical comrades attended him and a transport aircraft was summoned to take him and the other wounded back to England to be treated.

That was the end of Peter's war.

He was flown home to the United States in May 1945.

Turkey Enters the War

Chapter 22

1943

Winston Churchill had been pressing Turkey to declare war on Germany for some time, he stressed the need for a second front to be opened in the Balkans led by Turkish forces. Stalin and Roosevelt insisted the second front be opened through Normandy in France.

Turkey had resisted the call to allow British bases on Turkish soil arguing this would lead to Germany declaring war on the neutral state. Turkey also insisted she didn't have the resources to wage war unless the allies supplied adequate weapons. The shopping list Turkey presented would take several years for the Allies to provide.

Zehra and Emir were well aware of these discussions and negotiations. They were also cognizant of the fact that if Turkey did enter the war albeit at the final stages of the conflict their safety would be compromised living in German-occupied France.

The two diplomats would often dine at their favourite restaurant, Le Procope, on a Saturday night. They decided to try a new venue called La Petite Chaise. When dining out in Paris, it was important not to discuss anything political or controversial, as Gestapo operatives were prolific in the city.

'Well, darling do you see anything on the menu that looks interesting?' asked Zehra.

'I'm leaning towards escargot as an entrée and Sole Meuniere as the main course.'

'Have you decided?'

'Yes, I'm having Coquilles Saint-Jacques and Margret de Canard.'

'You always seem to choose duck.'

'And you always seem to choose seafood.'

'Oh well, it's better to eat something you know and like, although we really should be more adventurous while we're still living in Paris.'

'I know we can't discuss it now, but the rumour is we may be heading back home soon. Is that right Zehra?' said Emir.

'You're right we shouldn't discuss it now.'

The entrees arrived, both looked delicious. As they began their meals a Gestapo car screeched to a halt outside the restaurant. Four leather coated Gestapo officers jumped out of the black Mercedes and entered the restaurant. They approached a table, a family of two adults and three children, dragging them out into the street where a second car was waiting. The car sped off to Gestapo headquarters. The incident took only a few minutes. The remainder of the diners went back to eating their meals and drinking their wine as though nothing much had happened.

'Zehra, that family looked familiar to me, I think they may be on our list for the next train caravan.'

'Our next and possibly last. So, you think they may be Turkish Jews?'

'I can't be sure, but I intend to find out.'

'Emir, you must be careful you don't want to find yourself on a train to Poland again. The way things are I may not be able to rescue you next time.'

Emir excused himself and caught a taxi to the infamous Gestapo building located at 84 Avenue Foch.

Emir arrived at the Gestapo building at 11 pm. The typical Parisian exterior was in stark contrast to its real purpose. In this building torture and murder took place on a regular basis.

Holding Cells Below Gestapo Building

The Turkish diplomat entered the impressive entrance approaching the front desk. Emir introduced himself and explained his purpose. The officer instructed Emir to wait on the mezzanine floor while he spoke to his superiors.

After an hour of waiting a Gestapo Colonel approached him.

'I believe you are concerned about a Jewish family which has been hiding from the authorities for quite some time?'

'Well sir, I'm of the firm belief that family is Turkish and exempt from deportation.'

'Do you have any proof of their nationality?'

'Yes sir, I believe I do, although the papers are back at my embassy.'

'OK, go and get them and I will give your request to release them due consideration.'

'Thank you, I appreciate your cooperation.'

Emir caught another taxi to the Turkish Embassy just two blocks away. He instructed the driver to wait while he retrieved the appropriate immigration papers. It took some time to sift through the files but after thirty minutes he found the folder. Emir only had photos to identify them, as he was not aware of the family's name.

He was relieved to discover the taxi had waited. Emir returned to the Gestapo building and asked to see Colonel Iffinger. Again, he was instructed to wait on the mezzanine floor until the Colonel could see him.

Two hours passed, Emir was still pacing up and down the floor when finally Colonel Iffinger appeared.

'So Mr Saatchi, you have the necessary papers?'

'Yes Colonel, the family's name is Akkas, they immigrated to France in 1932.'

'Well Mr Saatchi, these papers seem in order. I'll give instructions to release the family to you.'

'Thank you, Colonel.'

Emir had waited another hour before the Colonel returned.

'I'm afraid we have a problem, the family is already being transported to Auschwitz in Poland, the train left two hours ago.'

'Well, can I get them off it before it leaves France?'

'I'm afraid not. I can't help you anymore.'

'But surely.'

'Mr Saatchi, that's the end of it. Please go.'

Emir knew he had lost this battle. He returned home to the embassy apartment very disconsolate. Zehra comforted him, but she knew her husband would take time to get over the harrowing experience.

Emir knew that the last opportunity to save his Jewish countrymen and women had passed. Turkey would soon become the enemy of Germany, and he and Zehra would need to leave Paris.

Churchill finally lost patience with Turkey's indecision, warning the Foreign Minister, Menemencioglu, that: 'Unless Turkey made use of its final opportunity to side with the future victors, it would be deprived of the chance to sit at the winners table later on, and all it would end up doing would be wandering along the corridors as a mere member of the audience'.

At the second round of the Cairo talks, Turkish President Inonu declared he would not be given orders from Churchill and insisted he should have an equal say.

He managed to convince Roosevelt and Churchill that Turkey would not be ready for a major operation planned to take place shortly.

1944

It became apparent to Germany that Turkey was becoming more closely aligned with the Allies.

President Inonu took measures to exclude those people who were known as Nazi sympathisers from official posts, in order particularly to appease the Soviet Union. First, Fevzi Cakmak was forced by Inonu to resign from the post of Chief of General Staff. Numan Menemencioglu, the Foreign Affairs Minister, shared the same fate.

President Roosevelt and Prime Minister Churchill demanded that Turkey ceases all commercial and diplomatic relations with the Nazi Germany. This Turkey did on 2 August 1944.

1945

In February 1945, Stalin, Roosevelt and Churchill met in the Crimean province of Yalta. Their primary aim was to determine the future of world order. One point on which consensus was reached was that only states at war with Japan and Germany as of 1 March would be invited to the San Francisco Conference which had been organised for the purpose of establishing the United Nations. Turkey severed her links with Japan on 6 January. Turkey officially declared war on the Axis powers on 23 February. However, the only motive behind this move was merely a desire to satisfy the 'procedural formalities' to join the newly formed United Nations. The country remained non-belligerent until 14 August– the day when the war finally ended with Japan's surrender.

I Still Call Turkey Home

Chapter 23

December 1, 1944

Emir was given the task to ensure all important files in the embassy were packed in boxes ready for transportation to Ankara. All the embassy staff were required to be ready to board a train bound for Istanbul on 15 December.

Zehra requested an appointment with Carl-Heinrich von Stülpnagel, Military Commander of Paris to inform him that the embassy had been closed by the Turkish Government on the basis of protecting its diplomatic staff from a possible Allied invasion of Paris.

The Military Commander assured Zehra that Paris was secure and that Germany was still confident of winning the war. Nevertheless, he understood she must obey orders; he wished her well.

December 15

The embassy staff and their families, forty people in all, assembled on platform eight. The locomotive with its ten carriages was waiting to take them back to Turkey. German officials checked all the passengers' passports; they were all in order. Once cleared the last train out of Paris headed for Istanbul Turkey then on to Ankara.

The journey was uneventful, the train made its way through Croatia, Serbia and Bulgaria without incident. This time, the train wasn't transporting Jews back to Turkey.

After three days the locomotive pulled into Sirkeci Railway Station in Istanbul. Zehra, and Emir were relieved to be back on Turkish soil as were the other passengers from the embassy.

Sirkeci Railway Station Istanbul

The Saatchis continued to Ankara the following day travelling on the same train that brought them from Paris. It was their intention to resign their commissions to the Minister of Foreign Affairs, Mr Hasan Saka.

Hasan Saka received the couple in his office, reluctantly accepting their resignations. He thanked the two seasoned diplomats for their dedicated service over the previous nine years.

Zehra and Emir were looking forward to returning to Tekirdag and their much-loved "Utopia" where they planned to extend and renovate the original farmhouse. Before departing Ankara they visited Mustafa's resting place inside the Ethnography Museum. Zehra's brother had died seven years earlier and had been placed in a white marble sarcophagus waiting to be transferred to the magnificent "Anikabir", a permanent tomb for the much loved "Father of the Turks". The mausoleum took fifteen years to construct.

Anikabir

Once all the paperwork was completed Emir and Zehra travelled by train to Istanbul where they purchased a new motor vehicle, a Rolls Royce. The decision was made not to buy a Mercedes this time after what they experienced and witnessed during their time in Berlin and Paris.

Despite having visited "Utopia" a number times over the past several years when they returned for brief periods the euphoric feeling of driving up the long tree lined drive was amazing. They were home at last and determined never to live anywhere else again.

No sooner had they returned home than they began planning the renovation of the farmhouse. They envisaged leaving the original house and building an L-shaped building beside it. One wing would comprise five additional bedrooms so that Zehra's nieces and nephew could become regular visitors along with their families. The other wing would include his and hers study and a large billiard room.

Building began March 1 and continued for six months. Building materials were in short supply as the war in Europe continued until May 8. Fortunately, the orchard had an abundance of stone the same type of stone used to construct the farmhouse.

Zehra was able to use her influence to secure the timber and roofing tiles required to complete the exterior.

The building was completed late September, and the dozen or so workmen could move on.

December 1945

The next project the couple had in mind was adopting a baby. Despite years of trying and endless medical tests for both of them Zehra and Emir couldn't produce a child.

They wrote to the adoption agency in Istanbul requesting an appointment they received a reply soon after. The agency suggested the two of them come to their offices at their earliest convenience to discuss options. Zehra telephoned the Director and made the appointment for Monday, October 25.

Zehra and Emir made the journey in three hours arriving at the adoption centre at 12 midday, thirty minutes early.

'I'm feeling nervous darling what if they decide we're not suitable to adopt?' asked Zehra.

'Don't be silly Zehra, course they'll accept us, we are ex-diplomats with a very successful business, besides you're Mustafa Ataturk's sister.'

'I suppose you're right, it's just that I want a child so much.'

'So do I my love. I promise we'll be parents very soon, you'll see.'

They entered the building holding hands both very pensive; they were ushered into a large office lined with mahogany panels, it was the Director's.

'Good afternoon Mr and Mrs Saatchi, please take a seat. I've read your application, and my department is fully supportive of you adopting a child. The only decision to be made is what child. I have had my staff prepare dossiers on several children that could be suitable.'

Zehra and Emir were shown the dossiers of eight children all under 12 months old. It was ironic they both chose the same baby, a boy.

The agency made arrangements for the new parents to return the following Monday to collect their new bundle of joy.

The name they chose was Maceo, meaning God's gift.

Zehra and Emir drove the three hours with great expectations, the agency had Maceo ready for the return journey. Zehra held her son in her arms for the entire trip, bottle-feeding him en route.

The new family arrived home at 5 pm. Maceo was sound asleep, they placed him in the cradle in the newly decorated nursery. Both mother and father couldn't leave the nursery for another half an hour, they just kept looking at him with total adoration.

Zehra decided it would be beneficial to have a nurse residing at Utopia just in case something went wrong or she needed help. The nurse's name was Esma, she was a local girl but trained at the Istanbul General Hospital.

December 1946

Life was good. Maceo was now eighteen months old, a very healthy happy little boy. Zehra was a full-time mother although still very much involved in running the business. Emir was back in control, however he decided to retain Beren and Karem as managers in "Arilik" as they had both proved their worth in his absence.

The little boy loved to walk through the apple and olive groves with his father, when the toddler became tired Emir would piggyback him for the remainder of the journey. His parents decided to ensure Maceo learnt English as well as Turkish, by the age of five he was fluent in both languages.

Arilik Olive Grove

Once Maceo began his schooling in Tekirdag, he met other boys his age. One particular boy, Hai, became his first best friend, Tabor was his second. The three boys would play tag and various ball games including soccer with the other boys in their class.

Under the management of Emir and Zehra, the agricultural business Arilik grew dramatically in the post-war years. The world was crying out for high-quality produce. New markets were opening including Great Britain, United States of America and Australia. To ensure the security of the marketplace Emir was required to travel often to visit his ever-increasing clientele.

Once a year the family would accompany Emir. This gave their young son an education that couldn't be achieved staying home in Turkey. Maceo visited the Tower of London, Big Ben and various other London landmarks. In America he got to see The Grand Canyon and ride to the top of the Empire State Building.

1956, Melbourne Australia

Emir and Zehra decided it was time to visit Australia and develop this growing market. The fact that the Olympic Games were being held in Melbourne was a bonus. Emir had not been back to his land of birth since he left its shores as a twenty-year-old soldier. They also planned to travel to Tasmania where his mother lived; Emir was eager to renew their relationship.

Maceo had never flown on a plane, he was excited by the prospect, however by the time they arrived in Melbourne he'd had enough of air travel.

Emir had organised tickets for the opening ceremony, swimming, day two of the athletics and wrestling.

Once they booked into the Windsor Hotel in Spring Street, they decided to have lunch in the dining room.

Windsor Hotel

The next evening the family headed for the Olympic Stadium to attend the opening ceremony, it was only a mile walk from the hotel.

They all enjoyed the spectacle, especially when the Olympic flame entered the stadium. It had completed a very long journey.

The Olympic Flame was relayed to Melbourne after being lit at Olympia in Greece on 2 November 1956:

Greek runners took the flame to Athens;

The flame was transferred to a miner's lamp then flown by Qantas Super

Constellation aircraft "Southern Horizon" to Darwin, Northern Territory;

A Royal Australian Air Force English Electric Canberra jet bomber flew it to Cairns, Queensland where it arrived on 9 November 1956;

The Mayor of Cairns, Alderman W.J. Fulton, lit the first torch;

The first runner was Con Verevis, a local man of Greek parentage;

The flame was relayed down the east coast of Australia using diecast aluminium torches weighing about 3 pounds (1.8 kg);

The flame arrived in Melbourne on 22 November 1956;

Ron Clarke lit the Olympic Flame at the stadium.

The Duke of Edinburgh opened the games on behalf of Queen Elizabeth.

The first event they attended was the swimming. Emir felt great pride seeing Murray Rose win the first of his three gold medals. Despite not having lived in Australia for over forty years he still felt Australian. Maceo wondered why his father was so excited by an Australian winning.

The Saatchi family attended Olympic events over the next five days. Zehra, although she had no interest in wrestling, was delighted that her country won three gold, two silver and two bronze medals all in wrestling.

Zehra, Emir and Maceo flew from Melbourne to Hobart, hiring a car and a driver to take them to Franklin where his mother resided at Elder Care.

Emir was extremely nervous about seeing his mother, it had been forty years, and despite sending her birthday and Christmas cards, there had been no contact.

When the family arrived at the aged facility, the manager informed them that Vera had been taken to hospital in Hobart suffering a severe fever.

Emir instructed the driver to return to Hobart, a fifty-mile drive, so that they could visit Vera at the Royal Hobart Hospital.

The receptionist told Emir that Mrs Vera Jacobson was not allowed visitors. Her doctor was called to explain the situation to the family in the reception area.

They left the hospital disappointed checking into their hotel for the night, the family would fly back to Turkey the following day.

Maceo was looking forward to returning home. It wasn't that he didn't enjoy his holiday in Australia however he was about to embark on a new life journey. Maceo was about to become a man.

Emir and Zehra had arranged Maceo's Sunnet party to be held at Utopia on February 1 when their son would be transformed from a boy to a man.

The Arabic word "Sunnet" means adherence to the teachings of the Prophet Muhammad. Sunnet translates to "busy path," which, in a broad sense, refers to the path to God. The word is not mentioned in the Koran, but it is mentioned in the "Sunnah", the record of the Prophet's words and deeds. The procedure is traditionally regarded as an important function of cleanliness. The fact that Emir was born Jewish meant he did not need to be circumcised when he converted to Islam.

Zehra and Emir decided they would have their son circumcised in a hospital in Istanbul rather than at a sunnet ceremony as he had a propensity to bleed easily.

Once the surgical procedure was completed they would hold a sunnet party at Utopia ten days later inviting about 200 guests.

The boys dress in special costumes, most commonly including a hat with the word, "Masallah" meaning "Wonderful. May God avert the evil eye," embroidered on the front.

Maceo in Sunnet Costume

Emir and Zehra decided they would purchase a sunnet ring for their son to commemorate his coming of age. Zehra's uncle had retired so they decided to visit the House of Khan. Emir had organised Saladin and his family to escape from Paris.

Emir chose the ring design on a previous trip to Istanbul. The three of them would go to the Grand Bazaar when Maceo was discharged from hospital.

The stone he chose was turquoise.

Maceo was pleased to leave the hospital, he was looking forward to the grand party where he would be the centre of attention.

The Istanbul Private Hospital was only two blocks from the Grand Bazaar therefore they decided to walk. As the family turned the corner into Keseciler Road leading to the market, they heard yelling and screaming.

Hundreds of Turks were chasing Turkish Greeks, bashing them and smashing shop fronts. The police were trying to stop the riot but weren't making much progress. Several gunshots rang out, no one was sure if they came from a rioter's gun or from the police.

Maceo dropped to the footpath, blood gushing from a head wound. His parents tried to stem the flow, but it was an impossible task. He died minutes later, still lying on the footpath.

When the fighting had subsided, an ambulance was called to take the fatally wounded boy to the hospital where a doctor, the same doctor who had performed the circumcision, pronounced him dead.

Zehra and Emir were devastated. Their only son, the boy they adopted only nine years ago, had been taken from them in such a horrific way.

Instead of Maceo's sunnet party the couple hosted his funeral. Two hundred friends and relatives attended.

Riot Aftermath

The Turkish Pogrom

In the 1950s Cyprus was one of the most significant national issues facing Turkey. A conference was held in London including Greece and Great Britain with the express purpose of establishing the status of Cyprus. Cyprus since time immemorial had been Greek, it was invaded in 1571 by the Ottoman Empire as part of the overall Islamic expansion. But the Muslim colonists had remained a minority, and were still so at the liberation of Cyprus during World War One and later at the collapse of the Ottoman Empire.

It was reported in Turkish newspapers that Greek terrorists had exploded a bomb in the birth house of Kemal Atatürk in Thessaloniki, Greece. On the same day, demonstrations broke out in Turkey led by students and thugs. Within two days practically the entire Greek population had been driven from their homes. The police openly supported the attacks; later it became known that the riots had been instigated by the Turkish secret police.

The disaster that struck the Greek population was of incomprehensible magnitude. Constantinople (Istanbul) had long been Greek and capital of the East Roman Empire, but was conquered by Muslims in 1453. More than 500,000 Greeks were still living in Constantinople in 1920. The assault caused almost all Greeks to lose their houses, businesses, companies and trades. Almost all churches were destroyed, as well as Christian institutions, general stores, schools, newspapers; cemeteries were systematically destroyed to erase any trace that the city had originally been Greek.

The material losses were:

Destroyed private homes:	2600
Destroyed shops:	4348
Destroyed hotels:	110
Destroyed pharmacies:	27
Destroyed factories:	21
Burned churches:	38
Destroyed churches:	35
Destroyed Christian schools:	35
Destroyed newspapers:	3

It was an horrendous riot that took young Maceo's life.

White Horse Black Dog

Chapter 24

Part of the Sunnet ceremony entails the young boy to ride a white horse through his local village. The villagers come out of their homes waving and singing as he rides through the streets dressed in his Sunnet costume.

Emir and Zehra purchased a beautiful pony for Maceo's ceremony. They arranged for their son to dress in his costume and ride the pony they named Guzel as a dress rehearsal for the big day.

After the funeral, Zehra and Emir were understandably morose, they had lost their only son to a stray bullet in what would be called later Turkey's ethnic cleansing pogrom.

Zehra coped by engrossing herself in the business. She felt if she were busy there would be less time to grieve.

Emir's behaviour was quite the opposite; he spent little time on business affairs and more and more time working in the orchard. When he wasn't pruning or weeding he would simply walk between the trees remembering the many times he spent in this serene environment with Maceo.

Communication between husband and wife became strained, no longer did they discuss their son's progress at school or his soccer skills nor did they discuss Arilik. Long periods of silence were the norm as opposed to the laughter and chatter they once enjoyed at the dinner table.

Both feared they would ultimately breakup and divorce.

Emir became more and more dark in his moods, he also found it difficult to sleep, four hours was now the norm.

They say time is a healer but that theory wasn't working for Emir.

As the months passed Emir was not demonstrating any signs of improvement. It was now obvious to Zehra that her much-loved husband was suffering from severe depression. She had suggested that Emir should obtain a referral from their local doctor to a psychiatrist in Istanbul, but he would not hear of it.

Emir was wandering through the apple orchard, he sat down leaning against one of the trees. Being amongst the trees reminded him of his boyhood home in Tasmania. He, his parents and his young brother all worked together at harvest time; it was laborious but enjoyable.

His train of thought drifted to his enlistment in the army with his best mate Frank, two blokes going off to an adventure of a lifetime. Emir recalled the horrors once he and Frank arrived on Turkish shores at Gallipoli. Neither of them was prepared for the disgusting carnage, the horrors of war. Neither he nor Frank left Turkey to return home to Tasmania, they remained on Turkish soil, he at Tekirdag and Frank at the beach cemetery on ANZAC Cove.

The thoughts of his family in Tasmania and losing his best mate didn't help Emir's depression; in fact he began to feel worse.

Emir walked back to the farmhouse. He entered the barn; the same barn where he had sought refuge from Turkish troops in 1916.

He opened the cupboard in the tack room, took out a rifle; the rifle he used as a crutch on his journey from Gallipoli. The German Mauser was in excellent condition. Emir cleaned it regularly and took it out into the orchard often for rifle practice.

He sat down with his back against a bale of hay, pointed the barrel under his chin. He hesitated but then having chanted 'Allahu akbar'. He pulled the trigger.

Catharsis

Chapter 25

Zehra had driven into the village to buy the ingredients for the night's dinner, a leg of lamb and several vegetables. Emir still loved a lamb roast, it reminded him of Sunday night dinners with his family in Tasmania. She also purchased a bottle of French wine, there was no need to buy beer as Emir had a stock of Fosters in the house. She enjoyed her trips into the village, she always ran into people she knew. What should have taken thirty minutes to do the shopping extended into a ninety-minute excursion chatting with friends and neighbours.

Zehra returned home to Utopia; checked the Aga stove to ensure there was enough heat, prepared the lamb and vegetables and placed the baking tray in the oven.

Aware that it would take ninety minutes she decided to go into her study and read some reports on the production levels of the dairy operation. Her General Manager was proposing they build a processing and bottling plant and create their own brand of milk as opposed to being just a wholesaler.

Zehra could see merit in the proposal but was concerned with the infrastructure investment required. She decided to discuss the proposal with Emir over dinner it may get his interest back.

Zehra looked at her watch it was 6.30 pm, the roast would be ready in 15 minutes. She returned to the kitchen, pulled out the tray, basted it and returned it to the oven. The bottle of wine had been corked earlier to let it breath, the only task left was to set the table, which she did with their finest crockery. Emir would typically return to the house thirty minutes before dining so he could share a drink with his wife and talk about the day. He was late; Zehra hoped he wouldn't be much longer, or the dinner would be ruined.

By 7 pm she became concerned, Emir was never this late. She was preparing to go outside to search for him when he walked in the door.

'Sorry darling, I know I'm late. I got caught up in something and time got away from me.'

'That's OK, but we need to eat straight away, we're having a lamb roast.'

'Ah, my favourite. Thank you, sweetheart.'

Emir had sat in the barn, the rifle between his legs. He pulled the trigger, but the gun had jammed. In over forty years the Mauser had never jammed. This was a sign from God he thought. He began to cry he realised if he had taken his own life his beautiful Zehra would be left alone; no husband, no son.

It was a cathartic moment. He promised himself he would get better; he would visit a psychiatrist and get help. Emir walked to the farmhouse feeling like he had been born again.

Over dinner they began to talk like they used to; openly and frankly.

'Zehra I've decided to see that psychiatrist you've been asking me to see. I know I need help to get through whatever it is I'm experiencing. I just want to be happy again.'

'I think that's a wise decision Emir, I know it must be difficult having depression. I'm still finding it very tough as well, but my love, life goes on.'

'Life goes on. How ironic, if she only knew,' he thought.

Zehra made the appointment for Emir to see their local doctor and friend Dr Ahmed Akkas. He wrote a referral to Dr Bozkurt, renowned as the best psychiatrist in Istanbul.

Emir drove to Istanbul to keep his appointment with Dr Bozkurt; the consultation rooms were in the old part of the city close to the Blue Mosque. He parked the car nearby and walked tentatively to meet with the psychiatrist for the first time. He was nervous; Emir wasn't one to open up or show his true feelings to people he knew let alone strangers.

He entered the waiting room and sat down; looking through the magazines on the table confirmed his theory that doctors wanted their patients to be bored while waiting to be seen. There was an assortment of very old Time magazines and various women's magazines, nothing that stirred his interest.

The doctor entered the waiting room. Introducing himself to Emir he then invited his nervous patient to join him in his office.

'Please take a seat Mr Saatchi.'

'Thank you, please call me Emir, after all, I get the feeling we will be spending quite a bit of time together.'

'Yes, we probably will. May we start by you telling me why you are here.'

'Because I suffer from depression.'

'What do you think causes you to suffer from depression Emir?'

'I lost my boy recently in very tragic circumstances.'

'Are you able to tell me about it?'

Emir described how a stray bullet had killed Maceo during the Greek riots three months before.

'Well, that would affect any parent severely. How is your wife coping with it?'

'With difficulty but better than me, she's a very strong woman.'

'Emir what goes through your mind when you are depressed?'

'Dark thoughts, very dark thoughts.'

'Have you ever contemplated suicide?'

'More than contemplated doctor I've attempted suicide.'

'When you say attempted what do you mean?'

'I mean I had a rifle up to my throat.'

'And at the last minute, you decided not go ahead?'

'No, I mean I pulled the trigger. The gun jammed, that's when I decided not to go ahead.'

'I see, how long ago was this?'

'Two weeks ago.'

'OK, Emir I'm sure we can work through this and 'tame the black dog' as they say.'

Emir visited Dr Bozkurt once a week for the following three months then once a month for another six. Throughout this period Emir gradually found himself again, he began attending board meetings and became an active member of the management team.

He naturally still missed his son terribly, but now he could cope with it.

As the end of 1959 approached, Emir was enjoying both his marriage and his business life. He and Zehra had constructed the milk and dairy processing plant and it was proving to be very successful.

The olive and apple orchards were producing record amounts of fruit, so much so that they expanded the olive oil plant, as well as the apple cider business.

Emir had returned from a business trip to Paris where he had negotiated a distributor agreement for Arilik Olive Oil. The French product would be called Purete–both Arlik and Purete translated to Purity in English.

He drove up the long driveway, a journey he never tired of, parking the car in the courtyard. Zehra came out of the house to greet him.

'Hello darling welcome home, would you like a coffee and a piece cake I just baked?'

'You know the way to a man's heart my love. Yes, I'd love a coffee. What sort of cake did you bake?'

'Your favourite, English Tea Cake.'

'Excellent.'

Husband and wife entered the house via the kitchen door Emir placed his briefcase on the floor sitting down at the long kitchen table.

'So, it was a successful trip darling?'

'Yes, very, I think the French market will be an excellent one for us.'

'Everything seems to be going well at the moment I hope it continues.'

'Course it will Zehra, we're doing all the right things.'

As Zehra brought the coffee pot and cake to the table, she stopped and grimaced; she just stood there with the look of pain on her face. Emir jumped up taking the coffee and the plate from Zehra's hands. He helped her to a chair and eased her down into it.

'Zehra, what's wrong darling?'

'I got a terrible pain in my stomach.'

'Have you experienced this pain before?'

'A couple of times.'

'Are you all right now? Has the pain gone?'

'It's easing, I'll be OK, probably something to do with change of life.'

'Do you think you should see Dr Akkas?'

'No, don't be silly darling, all women of my age suffer abdominal pain, it's just part of the process of getting older.'

'You're not old, and you're just as beautiful as the day I saw you in the barn all those years ago.'

'Thank you Emir, and you're just as handsome as that young Australian soldier I baled up.'

'Darling you have to promise me that if these pains persist you see Dr Akkas, you can never be too careful.'

'I will.'

'You promise?'

'I promise.'

What Zehra didn't disclose to her husband was she was experiencing other symptoms. Her stomach had swollen as though she was in the early stages of pregnancy, she also needed to urinate more frequently; a couple of times she didn't make it to the toilet in time.

She also felt tired during the day. When Emir was away she'd have naps in the afternoon. She never slept during the day before.

Life at Utopia went on Emir continued to manage and develop the business, Zehra attended board meetings and was active in the running of Arilik.

One Friday Emir arrived home parked the car and entered the kitchen to greet his wife. Zehra wasn't cooking, she was writhing on the kitchen floor. Emir knelt down on the floor assuring her everything would be OK. He raced to the telephone and dialled 112 for an ambulance.

The ambulance arrived from Tekirdag within fifteen minutes, transporting her to the hospital. Dr Akkas examined her initially. He ascertained her condition was serious and arranged for an ambulance to take her to the general hospital in Istanbul. What normally would be a three-hour journey took the ambulance two hours with its sirens going the entire way.

Zehra was admitted into the women's ward where a gynaecologist, Dr Husim, examined her. He instructed the nurse to administer a codeine-based painkiller. Once the codeine took effect, she was able to get some sleep.

Emir drove to the hospital the next morning in the hope he would be taking his wife back home.

A gynaecological oncologist Dr Parlak, visited Zehra the next morning. He ordered some tests to determine her condition. She and Emir had to wait three days before the test results came back.

The specialist was pleased that Emir had stayed in Istanbul while Zehra was in the hospital, he preferred to speak to both husband and wife at the same time. He entered Zehra's room just before lunch, accompanied by the gynaecologist who first examined her upon her admission.

'Good morning Zehra, how are you feeling today?'

'Better doctor, although I think the painkillers have something to do with that.'

'Yes, I'm sure you're right. We'll keep you on them for the time being. Hello, Mr Saatchi I'm glad you're here I prefer to discuss these matters when both spouses are present.'

'So, do you have the results of the tests doctor?' asked Emir.

'Yes, I do. I'm afraid it's not good news, you have ovarian cancer Zehra.'

'Oh my God, cancer!'

'Not what we were all hoping for but we need to take some affirmative action.'

'What action exactly?'

'We will need to operate and endeavour to rid your body of the disease.'

'What does that entail doctor?' asked Emir.

'We believe you are at stage 1B, let me show you on this diagram.'

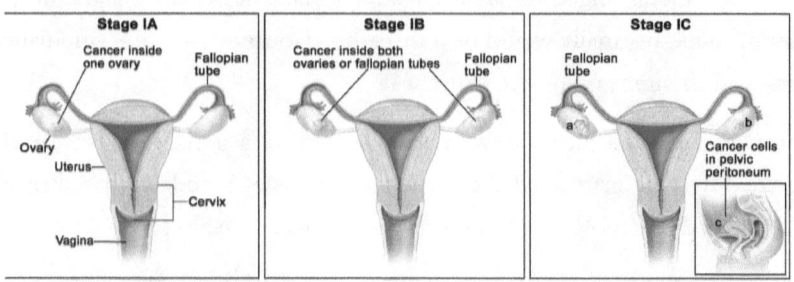

'As you can see the cancer has spread to both ovaries I'm unsure at this stage whether it has spread to the fallopian tubes. The good news is it hasn't metastasized to the bowel.'

'So what will you need to remove?'

'Both ovaries and fallopian tubes plus the womb, including the cervix. This operation is called a total abdominal hysterectomy.'

'Doctor you said you weren't sure if the cancer had infected the fallopian tubes, why take them out?'

'I'm afraid we need to be sure there are no cancer cells in the tubes removing them is the only way we can be sure.'

'Well, this is a shock. I don't know what to think.'

Emir was holding his wife's hand throughout the consultation. He was ashen.

'We need to book you in for surgery as quickly as possible Zehra. I've looked at my schedule and find I can perform the operation tomorrow morning.'

'That doesn't give me much time to prepare, I have an important business meeting tomorrow morning.'

'Don't worry darling, I can handle it. The most important thing is getting you curedm' said Emir.

'I suppose you're right darling it's just that it seems so rushed. To tell you the truth I'm scared.'

'Course you are, who wouldn't be? But you have the best surgeon in Turkey taking care of you. You'll come out of this fine then we'll go on that trip to Australia and New Zealand we've been planning.'

The Battle

Against the Enemy Within

Chapter 26

March 1960

Zehra had a restless night in hospital, as did Emir in the couple's Islamabad apartment. Both prayed to Allah for a satisfactory result.

At 7 am two nurses entered Zehra's room to prepare her for surgery. They scrubbed her down and dressed her in a surgical gown. Once that was completed, they wheeled her down in a gurney to operating theatre one.

It was quite daunting being wheeled into the operating theatre, the bright lights, the nurses and doctors busily getting instruments and equipment prepared. The nurses moved her over onto the operating table. Dr Parlak and Dr Husim smiled down on her.

'How are you feeling Zehra?'

'Scared, apprehensive and very nervous.'

'Don't worry, I'm sure everything will go well, I perform this procedure regularly.'

The anaesthetist injected the anaesthetic into Zehra's arm, she slowly drifted off into a deep sleep.

The operation went to plan, it concluded four hours later. The surgeon was quietly confident he had removed all the cancer.

Zehra woke in intensive care, not the most tranquil of places.

The next day she was moved back into her private room Emir was waiting to greet her, they kissed and held hands for hours.

Dr Parlak visited that night to check on his patient.

'How are you feeling Zehra?'

'Pretty good doctor I'm in no pain, but I suspect those marvellous painkillers are doing their job again.'

'We'll keep you in for four or five days to help you recover. I'll come in every day to monitor your progress and check your blood pressure etc.'

'Thank you for all that you've done Doctor, I appreciate it.'

'Don't mention it Zehra, I just did my job.'

After five days Zehra was given permission to leave the hospital. Emir wheeled her out in a wheelchair and eased her into the front seat of the car. Zehra said farewell to the hospital staff that cared for her so well.

Emir drove carefully and slowly back to Utopia. At one stage Zehra complained at the speed they were going.

'Darling I appreciate your concern, but I would like to arrive home before nightfall.'

'You can't be too careful my love, you must be very tender.'

Eventually the Rolls entered the driveway to Utopia. Zehra had never been so glad to see her home again.

Gradually over the next month Zehra regained her strength, resuming her usual regime including helping Emir manage the business.

April 1961

Zehra felt like she was back to normal, her energy levels were excellent, and she was looking for new opportunities for Arilik.

She and Emir were sitting at the dining table, the fire was permeating a warm heat. They had just completed their evening meal and were finishing the last of their wine, an Australian cabernet sauvignon.

'Darling I've been conducting some research and I believe I can increase our margins for the olive crop.'

'That sounds good to me. How much increase do you estimate?'

'About 300%.'

'What, the whole olive production? We would have to increase our prices significantly.'

'No, I don't mean the oil and fruit, we have to remain competitive. I'm suggesting a new line of product.'

'Oh, what sort of product were you thinking of?'

'Cosmetics.'

'You mean face creams and such?'

'Yes, and other items. I believe it could be a very successful product line.'

'Can you share your research with me? I'm intrigued.'

'Olive oil has countless cosmetic properties. It restores the moisture levels of the skin, thanks to the large amount of essential fatty acids present in olive oil. It reconstructs the skin cell membranes, thanks to the action of oleic acid. It can be used as body massage oil. It tones up the epidermis and keeps its firmness.'

Emir and Zehra decided after developing a marketing plan to create a new division within Arilik: Saatchi Olive Estate–Natural Olive Skin Care

Zehra appointed a graphic designer to create the logo and labels while Emir purchased the necessary equipment and appointed a supervisor for the construction of the factory.

A chemist was employed to develop the skin care products.

January 1962

The launch of Saatchi Olive Estate–Natural Olive Skin Care was scheduled for January 15 at the Neorion Hotel, regarded as one of Istanbul's finest heritage hotels.

The launch was a complete success with buyers not only from Turkey but Greece, Italy and France attending. The skin care range was an immediate best-seller for the company. Zehra and Emir were delighted with the response to the new cosmetic range.

The couple decided now was the time to take the trip to Melbourne and New Zealand.

Zehra was required to visit Dr Husim for six monthly check ups, her next one was due in the next few weeks. She telephoned his consulting rooms to make the appointment. She was concerned that her bowel movements were irregular. She had also developed a nagging cough, although she put that down to a cold she had over the later parts of winter.

Emir drove her into Istanbul and came with her to the appointment. He stayed in the waiting room reading out of date magazines.

'Good morning Mrs Saatchi are you feeling well?'

'Hello Doctor, yes reasonably well although I wish I could throw off this cough.'

'How long have you been coughing for?'

'I caught a cold last January, it didn't take long to go, but this silly cough has stayed with me.'

'I see, do you have any other problems?'

'My bowel movements have become very irregular.'

The doctor listened to Zehra's breathing through a stethoscope. Although a gynaecologist he knew what to look for.

'Zehra I'm going to send you to the hospital for some tests. I'm sure there is nothing to worry about but it's best we make sure.'

'Will it require me to stay overnight?'

'No, just a day.'

Doctor Husim was able to book Zehra in for the following day, which saved her and Emir another trip. They stayed in their apartment.

The couple arrived at the hospital at 9 am. Zehra didn't have to wait long, Dr

Husim took blood samples and conducted a series of tests, some were invasive.

She was also introduced to a pulmonologist Dr Uysal, he specialised in diseases of the lung. She underwent a series of X-rays.

At 4 pm they were free to leave the hospital. Zehra had an appointment at Dr Husim's consulting rooms in five days time. Dr Uysal would see her after the initial consultation with Dr Husim.

Zehra was pensive on the trip home. Emir tried to engage her in conversation relating to the launch of the cosmetic range to try and get her mind off her health issues. Zehra wasn't interested, she was deep in thought.

The next five days vacillated between periods of complete silence between the two of them to happy times drinking wine and beer on the patio overlooking the orchard.

The day came when they would hear the results of the tests. Both Zehra and Emir were very nervous, the drive to Istanbul seemed to take forever.

Dr Husim invited both of them into his office. This was unusual Emir thought, I'm usually left to wait outside.

'Please take a seat. I'm not going beat around the bush Zehra your cancer has metastasized to your bowel and your lungs.'

'Good Lord no, it can't be.'

Emir put his arms around his wife trying to console her while at the same time seeking to absorb what had just been said.

'Doctor you will no doubt have to operate again?' asked Emir.

'I'm sorry, the cancers have progressed too far for me to operate.'

'So what happens now?' asked Zehra.

'You go home and enjoy the time you have left with your husband.'

'How much time do I have?'

'I can't be precise, but I would estimate between three and six months.'

'I see.'

The couple left the doctor's office holding hands, both trying to hold back the tears.

Life for Zehra and Emir completely changed as the days turned into weeks and the weeks into months. Zehra's health declined. Emir was by her side cooking and caring for her in every way.

May 5, 1962

Emir's regular morning routine was to rise at 7 am and make a pot of tea. He would bring the pot and cups on a tray into the bedroom, gently wake his wife and pour her a freshly brewed cup.

Saturday, May 5 was no different except for the fact that he couldn't wake Zehra. She had passed away in the night, Emir had no idea at what time.

The distraught husband climbed back into bed, hugging the love of his life. He couldn't let go for what seemed hours.

He whispered in her ear 'Inna lillahi wa inna ilayhi raji'un' ('Verily we belong to Allah, and truly to Him shall we return')

Finally, he rose and called his good friend Doctor Babak Akkas; the doctor made the arrangements to collect Zehra and transport her to the funeral home. He drove to Utopia to declare Zehra deceased and sign the death certificate. Babak consoled his good friend as much as one can when their life's partner has departed.

The funeral was held the following Monday in Tekirdag at the Rustem Pasa Mosque, the same Mosque where they were married thirty-seven years before.

Emir whispered 'Rest in Peace my darling.'

He went home alone.

A Heavy Cross to Bear

Chapter 27

Emir tried to cope as best he could but it was proving to be very difficult. He had hired a housekeeper and cook so at least he didn't have to worry about such mundane things. He knew if it was left up to him he would starve to death.

All the trading divisions of Arilik were thriving. Emir was thankful he had such a strong management team and an excellent workforce. He only attended monthly meetings and even then he was an observer, rarely a contributor.

April 1963

Emir decided he would travel back to Australia and see his mother on her 100th birthday—it had been nearly fifty years since he had last seen her. He arranged for a travel agent in Istanbul to make the necessary bookings, he decided to travel first-class, after all he could afford it.

His mother's birthday fell on Anzac Day, 25 April. He always thought that was ironic.

He arrived in Franklin Tasmania only to discover Vera had died on her birthday.

After he left Paul his great nephew he drove back to Hobart. He had a few hours before his plane departed for Melbourne where he would then depart for Istanbul.

Hobart Cenotaph

Emir decided he would visit the Hobart Cenotaph and pay his respects to his mates who paid the ultimate sacrifice.

He was moved by the fact that 10 Tasmanian officers and 380 other ranks were killed at Gallipoli. He ran his eye down the list of names, he stopped at Private Frank Miller. A tear came to his eye. He'd been best mates with Frank since they were both in 1st grade at Huonville Primary School. He remembered the day at Anzac Cove Beach Cemetery when he discovered that his good mate had died.

There was a list of Missing in Action—a cold shiver went down his back, listed amongst the missing was Private Geoffrey Jacobson.

'It's a sad yet inspiring place isn't it?'

Emir was unaware there was anyone else at the Cenotaph.

'Yes, it certainly is.'

'Did you fight in the Great War?'

'I wouldn't call it great, but yes I did.'

'Where about?'

'Gallipoli.'

'You didn't get over to The Western Front?'

'No.'

'I'm sorry, I should have introduced myself. My name is Bob Webber. I was a Captain in the 15th Battalion.'

'Hello Bob, my name is Emir Saatchi.'

Emir realised this man was the officer who gave him the order to conduct the recognisance at The Nek where he was captured by the Turks.

'That doesn't sound like an Aussie name, sounds more like Turkish.'

'That's right, I'm a Turk.'

'Well, I'll be. You know what Emir?'

'What's that Bob?'

'I've only known one bloke who had a birthmark in the shape of a cross on his neck.'

'Is that right.'

'Yep and his name was Geoffrey Jacobson. A bloody good shooter was Geoff, unfortunately, he got killed in action. His body was never found.'

'Would you like to have a beer at the pub, Bob? I've got a story I'd like to share with you.'

Bob and Emir developed a rapport, which developed into a strong friendship. Once Emir returned home they would call each other regularly on the telephone and talk for ages.

Emir led a lonely life. He had lost all those who he loved, his wife, his son and now his mother. Although he still took an active role in the company monthly meetings it wasn't enough to keep him occupied. A friend had suggested he take up golf but after six lessons and twelve months of trying to master the game he quit.

Bob called his good friend with the news that he would be travelling to Turkey for the 50th anniversary of the Gallipoli landing. He suggested that Emir also attend. Emir suggested Bob arrive in Turkey a week earlier than he planned so Emir could show him the sites of Istanbul and spend a couple of days at

Utopia. Bob agreed and made the arrangements.

April 18 1965

Emir drove his BMW to Istanbul airport to pick up Bob the plane was on time.

'Welcome to Turkey Bob I hope you enjoy your stay here.'

'I'm sure I will Emir, what have you got in store for me?'

'Well, I figure you must be pretty tired after your long trip so I suggest we go back to my apartment and you can rest up for the remainder of the day, have a nap. Tonight I'm taking you to my favourite restaurant, Rumelihisari Iskele. It is magnificent, great food and an amazing location right on the river. Tomorrow we'll do some site seeing around Istanbul, visit the blue Mosque and Sophia etc. The next day we'll drive to my home at Tekirdag and I can give you a tour of the orchards and the manufacturing plants.

'On the 24th we'll drive to Canakkale and book into a beautiful boutique hotel called Hotel Des Etrangers.

'As you well know the following day is Anzac Day, we'll catch a bus to the memorial. I suggest we stay another night in Canakkale to give us time to reacquaint ourselves with Gallipoli and the fond times we spent there.'

'As if, Emir.'

'Just kidding Bob.'

'The last two days are up to you, we can either go back to Tekirdag or spend some more time in Istanbul.'

'It sounds like you've got my visit all sorted mate.'

'I want you to enjoy your time here Bob, this is now my country. I'm very proud of it.'

April 19

The boys got a reasonably early start. They walked the one kilometre to the Blue Mosque. Bob couldn't believe the size of the structure.

Both men removed their shoes at the entrance and entered the holy place. The carpet could cover a football field and the domed ceiling was spectacular.

'My goodness mate I've never seen anything like that before! What a magnificent place of worship.'

'It is, now we go to Sophia.'

'Bloody hell, this is bigger than the blue one! They certainly went for size back then Emir.'

'They did Bob, Sophia was initially a Christian church built in 550. The Ottomans conquered Constantinople in 1453 and converted it to a grand mosque. When we go inside you can still see Christian mosaics.'

Emir and Bob entered the mosque. Bob was in absolute awe of the domed ceiling and the intricate artwork surrounding them. Emir pointed out one of the Christian mosaics.

Emir decided he would take Bob to the Grand Bazaar, the largest enclosed bazaar in the world.

'Do you wish to purchase anything to take back to Tasmania Bob? We are about to enter the Grand Bazaar, you can buy pretty much anything here.'

'Well, yes, I was hoping to buy my wife some Turkish jewellery.'

'Ah, I know the perfect shop, the House of Khan. Saladin the jeweller is a very old friend of mine, he'll look after you.'

The two friends entered the vast market. There were people everywhere purchasing goods from clothing to food.

Emir led Bob to the street of Jewellery, hundreds of jewellery shops some large others tiny. Half way down they came across The House of Khan. The shop would be considered large but not the largest in the bazaar.

They entered the busy shop. Emir couldn't see his friend Saladin, he asked the girl behind the counter of his whereabouts. She introduced herself as Aysu; Saladin and Ruth's youngest daughter.

'I'm pleased to meet you, I don't recognise your name.'

'You may know me as Sophie; when my parents came back to Turkey they gave us Turkish names so as not to be conspicuous.'

'Ah, I see. Where have I heard that explanation before?'

'What do you mean?'

'That's the exact same words your father used to explain why he called himself Philippe when they first moved to Paris.'

'Oh, really? My father isn't here at the moment, can I help you with anything?'

'Yes, my friend wishes to purchase a necklace for his wife back in Australia.'

'What were you thinking of, silver or gold?'

'I was hoping to buy a turquoise necklace, what do you suggest?'

'I prefer silver with turquoise, but it's up to you.'

Bob chose a necklace he thought his wife Ann would like. They were just about to leave the store when Saladin and Ruth arrived. They were both excited to see their old friend, insisting the two men join them for coffee.

There was an excellent coffee shop in the next street. Once they placed their orders with the waiter they began catching up with each other's news. Bob had trouble keeping up with the conversation, they spoke in both English and Turkish.

Emir told his friends about the death of Zehra, they were both heart broken, they knew her well.

'Bob did you know if it wasn't for Emir my family would have all been exterminated at the hands of the Nazis in Auschwitz?'

'No, I didn't know that.'

'It's true. He and his beautiful wife Zehra not only saved us, they saved 20,000 other Turkish Jews.'

'How did you do that Emir?'

Emir gave Bob a brief explanation of their work at the Turkish embassy in Paris during the war.

'You never cease to amaze me mate.'

They all finished their coffee. Emir and Bob said their farewells and headed back to the apartment.

They ate a simple Turkish meal that night at a little restaurant close to Emir's apartment.

April 20

Emir drove Bob to Tekirdag. Once they arrived in the coastal town he drove down to the harbour to show Bob how pretty the town was. Emir recounted it was from the jetty that he set sail for Gallipoli to re-join the fray all those years ago.

They drove past the mosque where Emir married Zehra and where he farewelled her.

The next port of call was Utopia, his much-loved home in the hills overlooking the coast. As Emir drove up the beautiful driveway Bob was in awe, the homestead surrounded by olive and apple orchards.

Emir showed Bob his room in the guest wing, it was large with its own bathroom attached.

'This is a magnificent spread you have here mate, I had no idea how large it would be.'

'Yes, too big for one person, but I do love living here. The only downside is wherever I look memories of Zehra come flooding back.'

'Yes, I'm sure it's very hard, she must have been an incredible woman.'

'She was Bob, she certainly was.'

'So, what time is dinner Emir? I was hoping to take a little nap, it's been a long day.'

'Yes mate, you've got time, we don't eat until 7 pm.'

While Bob was napping Emir checked with his housekeeper Cila to see what she was cooking for dinner.

She had chosen kebabs with various side dishes including couscous with grapes and feta and spinach tabbouleh; a traditional Turkish meal. The host also checked the refrigerator in the billiards room to ensure there was plenty of Fosters cold. Emir chose a very good French wine he had been saving, 1952 Chateau LaGrange.

Bob showed his face at 6 pm feeling slightly better than he did when he first lay down on the bed.

'Hello sleepy head, how are you feeling?'

'Not bad, I certainly needed that shuteye.'

'I think the long haul from Melbourne is still catching up with you.'

'Yeah, you're probably right.'

'Can I interest you in a cold glass of Fosters?'

'You've got Fosters? Well I'll be damned.'

'I've been importing it for years. A man needs his Australian beer mate.'

'Well, in that case, yes, I'd love a glass or two.'

'Bob, have you even eaten Turkish food?'

'No, mate, I've eaten Chinese, Indian, Italian and Greek but never Turkish tucker.'

'Well, you're in for a treat, my housekeeper is a great cook.'

Bob did enjoy his dinner, in fact he requested seconds. Bob and Emir enjoyed a coffee and a malt whisky. After dinner they talked about their time at Gallipoli and how strange it would be returning to the battlefields.

Both retired for the night just after midnight.

The next morning after breakfast Emir walked his friend through the vast olive and apple orchards. Bob couldn't help but impressed. In the afternoon they inspected the crushing and bottling plants, again Bob was amazed at the size of the operation.

The following day Emir escorted Bob to the milk processing and bottling plant in the morning and the Angus cattle stud in the afternoon.

At the end of the day Bob had an understanding of just how big and diversified Arilik was.

The next morning they would drive to Canakkale to begin their Gallipoli pilgrimage.

Emir asked his friend if he would like to visit the ruins of Troy, it was only a slight diversion to their trip. Bob agreed enthusiastically, he was a student of ancient history having read Homer's the Iliad when he returned from the war.

Troy was aptly described as ruins, it was difficult to imagine these dilapidated walls of stone ever being a magnificent fortified city. There was a guide available and they took advantage of his vast knowledge of the ruined city and the history surrounding it.

Walls of Troy

Gallipoli Revisited

Chapter 28

Emir drove into Canakkale, parking the car outside their hotel where they were fortunate to find a hotel room. There was a great influx of visitors expected for the 50th anniversary of the landing.

The Australian Returned Services League (RSL) had organised 350 Gallipoli veterans to arrive at the cove by ship just as they did fifty years before.

A request was made to the Menzies Government to provide a grant of $20,000 to help fund the veterans to make the pilgrimage. Although the Minister for Veteran Affairs approved the grant the Prime Minister later withdrew it. The RSL raised the necessary funds for the very special trip.

On 24th April 1965 the Turkish liner *Karadeniz* was moored off the island of Lemnos. It began its journey to Anzac cove in the morning just as the troop ships HMAT Seeang Bee and Australind had done in 1915. The difference being in 1915 the ships were loaded with young men expecting an exciting adventure and itching for a fight. In 1965 the ship was loaded with old men full of horrendous memories of blood, carnage, flies, bully beef and cold tea.

April 25, 1965

The seas were smooth at Anzac Cove permitting the veterans to board the lifeboats and be transferred to the beach where over two thousand people were waiting to greet them. There was a mixture of Turks, Australian and New Zealand backpackers and Anzac descendants. Only seventy veterans came by water, the balance were bussed in from Port Gelibolu, inside the Dardanelles.

In 1915 there was silence except for the lapping of oars in the still water as the boats approached the shore. In 1965 there were loud conversations; there was a full moon unlike the original landing enabling the old diggers to identify familiar landmarks.

'There's the Sphinx, it hasn't bloody changed in all these years. I thought it might have eroded a bit by now,' said Archie Turbot 15th Battalion.

The boats were tied to a temporary jetty and the old soldiers were helped out and escorted up the beach to join their comrades.

Anzac Day 1965

Emir and Bob were in the hotel's reception area waiting for what Bob thought would be the bus to take them to the Anzac Commemorative Site. A black limousine with Turkish flags flying on each guard pulled up.

'OK Bob, our transport has arrived.'

'You're kidding, is this for us?'

'That's right, compliments of the Turkish Government.'

'How come?'

'Hop in, I'll tell you on the way. The President asked me to read Mustafa Ataturk's message to the Australian mothers who lost their sons.'

'Why you?'

'I was Mustafa's brother in law and a good friend. I was also a decorated diplomat saving many lives during the Second World War. I'm also highly regarded as one of Turkey's most successful businessmen. These are not my words, they are the words of Cemal Gursel our President. How could I refuse?'

'That's fantastic Emir, what an honour. Emir, have you thought about the prospect of your old comrades recognising you by your birthmark?'

'Naturally I have, I'm going to cover it with a bandage. If anybody asks me I'll say I had a mole removed. I'm also going to wear my Fez. This is the Fez Mustafa gave me to wear to my wedding, it means a lot to me.'

The Government vehicle arrived outside the commemorative site, the two veterans walked the rest of the way.

'Bob I have to join the dignitaries. I'll catch up with you after the service.'

'Fare enough Emir, good luck with it.'

At 5.30 am the sound of the catafalque party could be heard in the distance; the slow deliberate beat of a drum with four men and women marching to the monument.

The order of service:

- Introduction

- Catafalque party mounts

- Commemorative Address

- Hymn

- Mustafa Ataturk's Message

- Wreath laying

- The Ode

- The Last Post

- One minute's silence

- The Rouse

- The National Anthem

- Catafalque party dismounts

It came time for Emir to approach the lectern and read the words of his brother in law and past leader.

Those heroes that shed their blood and lost their lives ... You are now lying in the soil of a friendly country. Therefore rest in peace. There is no difference between the Johnnies and the Mehmets to us where they lie side by side here in this country of ours ... You, the mothers who sent their sons from faraway countries, wipe away your tears; your sons are now lying in our bosom and are in peace. After having lost their lives on this land they have become our sons as well.

The audience were moved by Mustafa's magnanimous words.

Bob had caught up with a number of old comrades, they agreed to meet at the gunfire breakfast immediately after the service. He couldn't find Emir anywhere. 'Probably catching up with his Turkish mates,' he thought.

Emir was actually walking along the cove heading for the beach cemetery to pay his respects to his old mate Frank.

The wooden crosses had been removed and granite tombstones had now replaced them. It was beautiful little cemetery, if cemeteries can be described as beautiful. Emir found Frank's grave and placed a red poppy at the base of the gravestone.

He walked back to the commemorative site hoping to find Bob. Emir found the marquee where the gunfire breakfast was being held. The smell of sausages and eggs was omnipresent. Bob spotted him and called Emir over to his table.

'You were great mate well done.'

'Not really, they weren't my words, I only read them.'

'You read them with feeling.'

'Thanks, Bob.'

'Emir I'd like you to meet a couple of mates who fought with me over here. This is George Russell; George this is Emir Saatchi.'

Emir remembered George; he was the bloke who helped his good mate John collect jam bombs when John got killed by a snipers bullet bringing them back to the Anzac's position. Emir felt it was sad that he couldn't acknowledge this old soldier as a comrade.

Emir shook George's hand and said 'pleased to meet you.'

Bob introduced Emir to a few other 15th Battalion warriors. Emir knew them all; none of them recognised him.

Emir and Bob returned to the hotel, this time they chose to travel by bus along with the other diggers.

The following day Bob and Emir returned to Anzac Cove to walk some of the trails they traversed back in 1915.

They decided to climb up to the Nek and Lone Pine where some of the worst fighting took place.

Emir and Bob began climbing up past the Sphinx reaching Plugges's Plateau and up through Monash Valley reaching Russell's top within two hours of hiking. The last time Bob climbed this route it took over a day.

'Funny how easy it is when you don't have the enemy firing at you,' Bob said.

The two old diggers were amazed how much war debris still remained. They passed countless ammunition boxes and jam tin bombs along the way. The trenches had collapsed but the odd bully beef tin could still be seen.

'I bet you haven't eaten bully-beef since you left this place, Bob?'

'No bloody way Emir, I'd never eat that shit again.'

The two men finally reached the Nek close to the spot where Emir had been captured. They sat on a rock and looked out over the rugged terrain to Suvla Bay.

'It looks beautiful now Emir, not like it was back then.'

'The entire peninsular looks serene.'

They made their way to The Nek and Chunuk Bair reliving the horrendous battle.

'This would have to be the most senseless battle of the entire war,' Bob said.

Bob and Emir then trekked down to the beach where they met their Turkish driver at the agreed time of 5 pm.

Both men concluded coming back to Gallipoli had been both a fulfilling yet sad experience.

Emir drove his good friend back to Istanbul the next day, they both agreed to stay in touch. Bob flew out back to Australia, Emir returned to Utopia.

Lonely and Blue

Chapter 29

As Emir drove back to his home he reflected on the week he had spent with Bob. Although he enjoyed the time with his old captain and friend he also felt a sense of sadness. Not because he wouldn't see his friend again for a considerable time, it was more reliving his experiences on that horrendous battlefield they called Gallipoli. Emir arrived back at 9 pm. There were no lights left on by the housekeeper, which meant he was forced to fumble around to find the keyhole in the back door. Once he managed to open the door and switch on some lights he looked in the refrigerator for something to eat. Fortunately, Cila had left a platter of cold meats, cheese and olives for him. She had also baked a loaf of bread.

Emir poured a glass of red wine, sitting down at the kitchen table he began eating from the platter.

This was the table where so many things had been discussed, and decisions made with Zehra over the years. The adoption of their son Maceo, most of the business decisions they took were first discussed at the kitchen table.

Now here he was in the dim light alone, drinking red wine alone, eating his supper alone, and soon to be sleeping alone.

Emir finished his glass and replaced the platter in the refrigerator to be consumed for the next day's lunch.

He prepared for bed. Climbing into the cold sheets he lay there for what seemed like hours. Finally, he dozed off.

Emir didn't attend monthly Arilik management meetings regularly anymore, he found them too distressing without Zehra's presence. He tended to spend most of his daylight hours aimlessly wandering through the orchards. On several occasions, he discovered diamonds but didn't bother to pick them up, he didn't need the money.

At night, he sat in a leather armchair drinking Raki, a liquor he had never had a taste for in the past. He was now getting close to drinking as much as Mustafa had done when he was alive.

Emir knew he had developed depression again but didn't really care, over the following months his mood became darker and darker.

After he had drunk sufficient Raki he would become tearful, he missed Zehra and Maceo terribly and he wasn't sure if he wanted to continue living.

October 1, 1967

Emir woke to a dreary wet day, not the weather to lift one's spirits. He made his breakfast, consumed two cups of coffee and headed outside. He entered the barn, the place where his new life began in 1916.

He retrieved the Mauser rifle. Once again he sat with his back against a hay bale, held the rifle between his legs with the barrel against his chin.

He pulled the trigger. This time, the gun didn't jam.

RIP Emir.

The Aftermath

Chapter 30

Cila arrived at Utopia to prepare Emir's evening meal. She knew he had been feeling down so she decided to cook a lamb roast. Emir would always appear at 6 pm expecting his meal would be on the table. When 7 pm ticked over on the kitchen clock she decided to go and look for him. She walked around the grounds calling out his name but received no response. Finally, she entered the barn; she screamed and ran back to the house to telephone the police.

Two police officers appeared soon after, concluding it was suicide. The funeral home was contacted, they arrived soon after and took the body away to be prepared for burial.

Emir was buried two days later. Over two hundred people attended including the President and a number of Government ministers.

The estate was valued at US$100,000.000.

Emir's will specified that 50% of Arilik would go to the management and employees of the company based on years of service.

The RSL in Australia and the Turkish Veterans Association would each receive 12.5%

The remaining 25% would go to his only living relative Paul Jacobson.

The End

Epilogue

Mustafa Kemal Ataturk's Legacy

In 1911, Italy fought against the Ottoman Empire for the possession of what was then a part of the Ottoman Empire: Libya. Italy won this war, which demonstrated again the weakness of the Ottoman Empire. Bulgaria, Serbia, and Greece wanted the Ottomans out of Europe, and they overcame their differences as to how Ottoman holdings in Europe were to be divided. Bulgaria and Serbia were demanding autonomy for Bulgarians and Serbs within the empire, and Greece was calling for the liberation of oppressed Christians–Greeks–living within the Ottoman Empire. Montenegro joined in the opposition to the Ottoman Empire, and in October 1912, these four powers mobilised for war, for territory they believed was theirs. Germany backed the Ottoman Empire, and France backed Serbia.

In January 1913, Ismail Enver, one of those who had participated in taking power in 1908, led another coup. He had been a progressive military officer and one of the revolution's heroes. Now he bore the title of pasha and was Enver Pasha. He and his clique put aside the revolution's early ideology and claimed absolute power. Enver led an army to defend the empire's control over the city of Edirne, just inside Europe in Thrace. Bulgaria, Greece and Serbia began fighting among themselves, and the warring ended with Enver's regime still in control of Edirne but exhausted from war. The Enver regime was forced to give up control of territory that was to become Albania. The empire had lost control over Macedonia, and Salonika came under Greek control after 482 years of Ottoman control of that city. The Ottoman Empire now extended into Europe only as far as Edirne.

Elections were held in the winter of 1913-14, but opposition parties did not participate, and the new parliament was docile to Enver and what was still called the Committee for Unity and Progress (CUP).

With the outbreak of Europe's Great War in August 1914, Enver saw an opportunity to take back Islamic lands that had been absorbed by one of the belligerents–Russia. Enver dreamed of reinvigorating the Ottoman Empire. He feared that if Britain, France and Russia won against Germany and Austria-Hungary, they might deprive the empire of more of its territory. So Enver led Turkey into the war on the side of Germany.

Turkey helped the Germans bombard Russia on the Black Sea; Russia declared war on Turkey on November 2. France and Britain declared war on Turkey on Nov 5, and Britain found this an opportune time to cut the pretence that the Turks ruled in Cyprus and Egypt–lands that had been nominally a part of the Ottoman Empire but under British authority.

The Turks closed the straits between the Mediterranean and Black Seas, preventing Russia from exporting wheat by way of the Mediterranean Sea or receiving shipments of materials from its allies. To protect its oil wells in the Middle East, Britain moved a military force up the Persian Gulf to Iraq–part of the Ottoman Empire–where it began engaging Turkish forces. And in December, the Turks began an assault into Russia's Caucasus Mountains.

The Turks suffered a disastrous campaign in the Caucasus, and wartime passions and scapegoating led to the massacres of Armenians–despite the original respect for minorities by the Committee for Unity and Progress. During war enemy categorising came more easily, and for many among Turkey's Muslims, the war appeared to be against Christians–no matter that they were allied with Germany and Austria-Hungary.

German generals were with the Turks, directing the war effort, but with crucial help from one of Turkey's better generals, Mustafa Kemal, the Turks drove the Allies from the Gallipoli Peninsula, successfully defending their capital.

Meanwhile, the Turks were failing militarily in the empire's Islamic lands to the south. Enver had hoped that the Egyptians would rally behind the war effort on the side of Islamic unity. Sultan (and caliph) Mehmed had declared a holy war (jihad), but despite Ottoman propaganda about Islamic unity, the impact was minimal. The Arabs revolted against the Ottoman Empire in 1916. In January 1917, the British drove the last of the Turkish forces from Egypt, opening the way for a British advance to Gaza. In March, the Turks pulled out of Baghdad, and the British moved in. In July, an Arab force with Lawrence of Arabia took control of Aqaba (on the gulf coast at the southern tip of Jordan).

In Turkey, corruption was on the rise among the newly rich, with people selling transportation permits and speculating in goods, which the government was supposed to have requisitioned for the public. The public was growing demoralised and hostile toward the Enver government.

Enver was putting more hope in a German victory, but in the fall of 1918 the Germans were falling back on the Western Front in Europe, and under German generals, the Turks were falling back on the Southern Front. The British in early October seized Damascus and Beirut. The war appeared lost, and Enver and his associates stepped down from power around October 8, with Enver not staying to see what the Allies would do with him. Sultan Mehmed V had died in July, and on October 30th, the Ottoman Empire under a new Sultan Mehmed VI and a new cabinet led by Izzet Pasha agreed to an armistice. And this left the Allies believing they were in a position to do what they pleased with the defeated Ottoman Empire.

Turkey's Struggle for National Independence

Feeling empowered by their World War victory, the Allies wanted to end the Ottoman Empire–which had dared to join Germany in the war. The British, French, Italians and Greeks manoeuvred for advantage in the empire's breakup. The British occupied Constantinople and were manoeuvring to hold on to authority in Palestine and Iraq. In late March 1919, the Italians landed a force at Antalya, on the Mediterranean coast in south-western Turkey, and Italian detachments moved 100 miles northeast to Konya and over 150 miles westward to the coastal town of Bodrum on the Aegean Sea. The French landed in the extreme south-east of Turkey, along the Mediterranean in the region of Cilicia. There they supported the Christian Armenians who were taking revenge upon the Muslim Turks, while educated Turks were mysteriously disappearing. The French were advocating the closure of all Turkish primary schools, the revival of old mosque schools, and colleges establishing instruction in French. And the French were manoeuvring to take over Syria and Lebanon.

Mehmed VI, Islam's 100th caliph, and the empire's last Sultan. Turkish nationalists disliked his acceptance of the peace treaty and submission to Allied authority.

In Constantinople, Sultan Mehmed VI and government ministers submitted to the authority of the Allies while some Turks, inspired by President Woodrow

Wilson's Fourteen Points, were opposed to what the Allies were doing and were still looking with hope to the United States. They were especially inspired by Wilson's 12th point, which read:

The Turkish portion of the present Ottoman Empire should be assured a secure sovereignty, but the other nationalities which are now under Turkish rule should be assured an undoubted security of life and an absolutely unmolested opportunity of autonomous development.

The greatest irritant to the Turks was the Greeks taking what they saw as their territory. During the war, the British had promised the Greeks land in Turkey in exchange for entering the war on their side. The Greeks had accepted the British offer looking to a Greater Greece. The Greeks wanted the area around Edirne, western Asia Minor and the area of Pontus in Turkey's northeast–areas with sizeable Greek populations since ancient times. And Greeks looked forward to taking control of Constantinople, the former seat of Greek Orthodox Christianity.

At the Paris Peace Conference, the British advocated giving the city of Smyrna and its hinterland to the Greeks. The US and French delegations agreed, seeing such a move as protecting the Christian (Greek) minority in this region against the "murderous" Turks.

The Greeks landed near Smyrna in mid-May 1919, and bloody fighting erupted between them and local Turks. The Greeks sent the Turkish majority fleeing, leaving the area predominately Greek. The Greeks were now joined with the French and Italians in occupying a portion of Asia Minor.

On March 20, 1920, the official occupation of Turkey began with the arrival of British troops at Constantinople. British soldiers killed any Turks who resisted militarily, as one would expect of any military operation. But they also raided and closed Turkey's parliament and arrested and deported parliament deputies.

The Sultan and his ministers remained submissive. The government in Constantinople began persecuting those they perceived to be troublemakers, including those calling for the application of Wilson's Fourteen Points. The Sultan's government cooperated with Britain in the shipping of parliament's deputies and others to a prison on the British-controlled island of Malta.

Opposition to the impositions of the Allies and to the Sultan and his government began to form around the Turkish military leader, Mustafa Kemal. Having led the resistance to the Allies at Gallipoli during the Great War he had prestige among his fellow Turks. Since 1905 he had been a critic of rule by the Sultans. He had been a member of the military conspiracy that took power in 1908 but had been outside the inner circle and a thorn in the side of the Enver government during the war–Kemal not having favoured entering the war on Germany's side or fighting and dying for German interests. Now Mustafa Kemal was the foremost defender of Turkish nationalism and foremost Turkish opponent of the Sultan's government in Constantinople. Kemal was not a man easily intimidated or ready to surrender to the authority of the caliph.

Kemal was an aggressive organiser, and patriotic Turks rallied around him. In unoccupied Turkey, a National People's Congress was formed, which on April 23, 1920, elected Kemal as president. The new regime was centred in the town of Ankara. In Constantinople, Sultan Mehmed followed British pressure and denounced the nationalist movement, and an authority in the person of Sheik-ul-Islam denounced the nationalist movement as contrary to Islam.

What mattered more than Sheik ul-Islam's pronouncements was the military strength that the upstart regime under Kemal was organising. Turkey's military had been shattered by the war. Here and there outside the capital were units still intact but under strength. Civilians had taken up arms to defend their homes from the Greeks, and on 16 May 1920 Kemal began organising all irregulars into a force under his command. Some other generals joined their units to Kemal's forces. Turks were willing to pay what was needed to equip their military with adequate supplies, and soldiers under Kemal's command acquired a new hope and spirit. They believed in what they were fighting for.

On 10 August 1920, the Allies imposed upon the Sultan's regime the Treaty of Sèvres, which limited Turkey to a military force of 50,000–a force that was to be subject to "advice" from the Allied powers. The treaty gave Britain, France and Italy control over Turkey's financial affairs and granted to France and Italy their zones of control and influence. The treaty also granted autonomy to the Kurds. But Kemal's regime in Ankara refused to recognise the treaty.

The Allies saw Greek forces in Turkey as an instrument to enforce the Treaty of Sèvres. Kemal let the Greeks advance, giving the preservation of his troop's priority over holding territory. He was still building up the strength of his forces, while the Greeks were spreading themselves thin and extending their supply lines.

The first check to the Greek advance was at the Battle of Sakarya, between 24 August and 16 September 1921. The morale of the Turkish nation soared at Kemal's victory, adding to Kemal's strength.

In August 1922, with the Greeks as close as forty miles to Ankara, Kemal began a counteroffensive that sent the Greeks reeling back. Within two weeks the Greeks had their backs against the Aegean Sea. The British were unwilling to intervene with their own troops. The British public had had enough of war in recent years, and the issue of war against the Turks helped to drive from power the champion of the Greek cause, Prime Minister Lloyd-George. The Greek dream of a Greater Greece was shattered. The remnants of the Greek army had to be evacuated by sea, and much of the Greek population left with them, leaving an underpopulated Turkey and moving to an overpopulated Greece. A Greek presence in Asia Minor that stretched back thousands of years had come to an end.

Facing the military power of a united Turkish nation, the British evacuated Sultan Mehmed VI on 7 October 1922, taking him and his entourage by warship to Malta. The Sultan, in his sixties and still caliph, took with him his eighteen-year-old bride. The girl had been engaged to a navy captain. She was the daughter of the Sultan's gardener, and the Sultan had pressured the father into giving him the girl, against her will.

On November 2, 1922, the National Assembly in Ankara declared the old Sultanate abolished. Gone too were the leaders of the military coup of 1908 and the wartime leaders including Enver Pasha. Enver had asked Kemal permission to return. Kemal had refused and Enver had died at the age of 40 in August 1922 in an armed struggle against a Bolshevik army in what today is called Tajikistan.

In July 1923 at Lausanne in Switzerland the British, French, Italians, Romanians and Greeks signed an agreement with Kemal's government that recognised Turkey's independence and its permanent borders. Kemal's government agreed that the straits between the Mediterranean and the Black Sea would be demilitarised. There was an agreement to a temporary ban on increasing customs duties, an agreement that non-Muslim children in Turkey have available to them instruction in their own language and that non-Muslims would receive an equitable share in benefits provided by Turkey's national and local governments for education, religion, and charity.

Turkey was proclaimed a republic on 29 October 1923, and the nation rejoiced. Mustafa Kemal had led the Turks from occupation by the hated Allies and the ashes of the old Ottoman Empire to a new nation.

Secularisation

Mustafa Kemal had been urging Muslims to learn trades traditionally reserved for non-Muslims—shoemaking, tailoring, carpentry, tanning, blacksmithing and shoeing of horses. He wanted his fellow countrymen to open their minds to the most advanced learning, including science. Kemal's government began to reform education. Primary education was declared compulsory. From grade school to graduate school, education was to be free, secular, and coeducational, with the education of females equal to that of males.

Kemal had seen religious schools in Turkey bogged down in the teaching of Arabic by people who did not themselves understand the language. People who want to learn Arabic, he said, should study that language in Syria, Arabia or wherever it is commonly spoken. This did not sit well with those who favoured students speaking Arabic because it was Islam's holy language—even though the students did not understand what they were saying.

Kemal was less interested in defending Islamic tradition than he was in economic development. "The economy," he said, "is everything. It is the totality of what we need to live, to be happy."

Kemal had already proclaimed Islam to be the state religion. He wanted Islam to be a private creed, separate from government authority or economic influence. A conflict was brewing concerning the caliphate. With the sultanate abolished the caliphate had passed to Abd al-Majid, the former sultan Mehmed's cousin. Many in Turkey still saw the caliphate as equivalent to the head of state—while the relationship between the caliphate and the National Assembly remained unclear. Kemal did not want a caliph as a rival influence and slowing down his advances in education. The National Assembly proclaimed Turkey a republic on 29 October 1923. In March 1924 the National Assembly abolished the old dynastic way of transferring power and authority. It exiled from Turkey all members of the Ottoman (royal) dynasty—the family that had ruled over Ottoman territory for 625 years. The republic's constitution, created in 1924, left the National Assembly as the only legitimate representative of the sovereign will of the nation, and the National Assembly abolished the caliphate.

Destruction of the old Islamic order disturbed conservative Muslims inside Turkey and offended Muslims outside of Turkey. In Turkey, the government acquired more enemies. Many in Constantinople who had been attached to the splendour and glory of the Ottoman family were now enemies of the government. So too were tens of thousands who had been civil servants in Constantinople and disliked the capital having shifted to Ankara and their loss of jobs. Newspapers in Constantinople joined the conservatives and attacked the government in Ankara.

Adding to the unrest was a breakdown in relations between the government and Turkey's Kurdish population. Kurds felt linked to the caliphate. With the caliphate gone their bond with the state was broken. The government alienated the Kurds further by making them a part of the Turkish nation. The public use of Kurdish and the teaching of Kurdish were prohibited. Kurdish tribal chiefs and other influential Kurds were resettled in western Turkey. And Kurdish resistance was met by governmental repression.

Here and there devout Turks rioted. Kemal and his political party, the People's Party, were determined to maintain law and order. The People's Party controlled the National Assembly, and in March 1925 the National Assembly passed a "Law on the Maintenance of Order." Kemal's People's Party saw itself as struggling for survival amid hostile reactions to change, and it kept rival political parties suppressed.

In a further effort to secularise society, the National Assembly closed religious shrines and Dervish convents. And Kemal moved to abolish the hat called the fez. The Turks had been wearing western clothing for more than a century, but they had kept the fez as identity with Ottoman rule and as a religious identity. To wear a Western hat had become a symbol of separation from Islam. Despite the repressions then taking place under Kemal's rule, he believed that persuasion and public opinion was where the strength of reforms would ultimately lay. He journeyed to the most conservative of Islamic communities, in Kastamonu, and presented the community's religiously conservative notables with western hats. He argued with them, explaining that the fez was of Venetian origin, introduced by Sultan Mahmud II to do away with the turban, and he spoke of the greater practicality of hats with a brim. He succeeded. The conservatives went about town in their new hats–gifts from their esteemed president–and this led others in town to accept Western hats. And the new fashion in hats spread rapidly through the rest of the country, accompanied by the government banning the fez in November 1925.

In 1926, Kemal's government initiated judicial reforms. It replaced religious courts with Swiss and Italian penal law rather than Islamic law–the Sharia. Previously, theologians had had a monopoly on the legal profession. Now, only those who had studied Western law could pass the bar examination. Also in 1926, the government replaced the Islamic calendar with the calendar used in the West.

In 1926, an attempt was made on Kemal's life, with the planned assassination accompanied by plans for a coup d'etat. Many were arrested, including former politicians. Four were hanged and others sent to prison.

Mustafa Kemal was re-elected president on November 1, 1927. The National Assembly In 1928 moved in favour of improved literacy and comprehension at the expense of the use of Arabic. The Arabic alphabet was replaced with Latin symbols, with some Turks learning for the first time the association between pronunciation and letter symbols. The Koran was translated into Turkish and the new alphabet and Kemal spoke in favour of mosque sermons being delivered in a language that people understood: Turkish rather than Arabic.

In 1929, the government felt secure enough to let the Law on the Maintenance of Order lapse. Kemal supported the creation of an opposition party–a loyal opposition such as exists in Britain and the United States, but it was too much an imposition rather than a rise from opposing interests, and the attempt came to nothing.

In 1934, the National Assembly abolished the veil, the veil had been worn by married women of rank in pre-Islamic Arabia. With the spread of Islam, its use had spread among women in cities but not among nomads and farming people. Its use was not explicitly ordered in the Koran, but it had become identified with Islam. Under Kemal, the abolition of the veil was widely accepted and dismissed as a nuisance and Turkey's government saw the headscarf as a symbol of political Islam. Government regulation banned the headscarf from public buildings, including universities, its use to be preserved for religious services.

Women now had the vote, and they were now active as teachers, lawyers, doctors, and office workers and as members of the National Assembly. In 1934, polygamy was abolished, and for the sake of equality titles such as bey, pasha and others were abolished—titles that had gone to the highest bidder. And Turks were ordered to choose a family name. Previously Turks had one name given at birth usually associated with the faith, such as Muhammad, and another name was adopted in later years associated with their deeds or an admired person, as was the name Kemal. Mustafa Kemal was now given a grand surname, Ataturk, which meant father of the Turks.

Bibliography

http://ebookfriendly.com/most-popular-book-genres-infographic/

http://www.everyculture.com/To-Z/Turkey.html

http://www.nzhistory.net.nz/media/interactive/gallipoli-casualties-country

https://en.wikipedia.org/wiki/Military_career_of_Mustafa_Kemal_Atat%C3%BCrk#Sinai_and_Palestine_Campaign.2C_1917.E2.80.931918

http://www.turkeyswar.com/whoswho/who-mustafakemal.html

http://www.fsmitha.com/h2/ch09tu-3.htm

https://www.finebooksmagazine.com/press/2014/05/bonhams-presents-historic-wwii-artifacts-to-honor-70th-anniversary-of-d-day.phtml

http://www.ebay.com.au/itm/-/322150123778?

http://www.mrdowling.com/608-ataturk.html

http://www.columbia.edu/~sss31/Turkiye/ata/hayati.html

https://en.wikipedia.org/wiki/German%E2%80%93Turkish_Non-Aggression_Pact

http://sefarad.org/lm/044/5.html

http://www.raoulwallenberg.net/highlights/turks-saved-jews-nazi/

http://www.hup.harvard.edu/catalog.php?isbn=9780674368378

http://www.turkeyanalyst.org/publications/turkey-analyst-articles/item/367-hitler%E2%80%99s-infatuation-with-atat%C3%BCrk-revisited.html

https://jewishinfonews.wordpress.com/2009/09/01/turkey-and-the-holocaust-how-turkey-saved-jewish-lives/

http://www.thedailybeast.com/articles/2014/11/24/the-20th-century-dictator-most-idolized-by-hitler.html

http://adst.org/2013/06/the-nazis-take-paris/

https://en.wikipedia.org/wiki/Paris_in_World_War_II

https://www.washingtonpost.com/opinions/a-history-of-paris-during-nazi-occupation/2014/08/29/fce9e112-222c-11e4-958c-268a320a60ce_story.html

http://www.beautifulislam.net/judaism/turkey_holocaust_p.html

http://www.allempires.com/article/index.php?q=turkey_modern

https://en.wikipedia.org/wiki/List_of_Ministers_of_Foreign_Affairs_(Turkey)

http://www.pappaspost.com/unbelievable-photos-turkish-riots-greek-community-istanbul-1955/#slide-14

http://www.we-love-melbourne.net/1956-summer-olympics.html

http://www.turkeytravelcentre.com/blog/turkish-circumcision-ritual-party-sunnet/

http://traveltips.usatoday.com/turkish-sunnet-festival-100369.html

https://ovariancancer.net.au/awareness/what-is-ovarian-cancer/

http://www.womenscancerfoundation.org.au/personal-stories

http://www.cancerresearchuk.org/about-cancer/type/ovarian-cancer/treatment/surgery-for-ovarian-cancer

https://en.wikipedia.org/wiki/Category:Turkish-language_surnames?from=P

http://www.esenciadeolivo.es/en/the-culture-of-the-olive-tree/products/

http://insidestory.org.au/letters-from-a-pilgrimage

http://whc.unesco.org/en/list/849

https://www.awm.gov.au/sites/default/files/orders-of-service-anzac-day-2015.pdf

http://www.iwm.org.uk/history/20-remarkable-photos-from-gallipoli

Copyright

Serendipity: A Gallipoli Love Story is a work of fiction. Any resemblance to real persons, living or dead, is purely coincidental.

www.ingramcontent.com/pod-product-compliance
Lightning Source LLC
Chambersburg PA
CBHW020838260626
47169CB00003B/1045